EVERYTHING IS GREEN

Jim Kirk

Cover art by Jim Kirk

It is the end of winter and the cattle are out grazing the streets again. I stop to watch them on my way home from the grocery store. White, walking wrinkled fat sacks. It sickens me that I must enter their world just to fill my belly. Otherwise I would never leave the house.

My parents died two years ago from the virus. I live alone in the house that they left to me. I have no other family. I loathe friendships. I spend much of my time online talking to women. Nothing sexual, just for the company. I prefer the words of strangers. No expectations, no obligations. You can open your soul to them and they'll listen. It is my weakness that I still have the need for some human contact.

I was educated by the Jesuits. Many fond memories from that time, staying up all night reading and studying. It gave me little time to indulge in other pursuits. Now I have nothing but time, or rather the time I have left before I grow old and become infected. The prospect of death doesn't bother me. It is inevitable.

It is Monday. No one is online and I am left to my devices so I sharpen my knives and continue working on my wooden sculptures. My father set up a work station for me in our basement. He was a good man, an architect, and leader in the community. When I was a boy he was my hero, and I spent much of my life trying to emulate him, but now he is gone, along with my mother.

I would rather not talk about mother at this time except to say that we had a complicated relationship.

At night I practice my writing or watch the television. It was around the time of the outbreak that I became interested in serial killers, and I became a voracious viewer of documentaries on the subject. Ed Gein is my favorite. He was a master craftsman. I can relate to him on that level. I like to draw whimsical sketches of furniture made from human body parts. It is how I have fun in my lonesome world.

I prefer to be alone, though loneliness often follows. I watch the dog walkers through the windows of my living room. I like dogs, especially Rottweilers. I prefer the dogs to the walkers. There is a high school across the street and every weekday at 2:30 pm the good students walk home. At 4 pm the bad students who served detention get out. Was I ever that young? I look in the mirror and count the gray hairs in my beard, and the bags under my eyes.

Today a religious person knocked at the door and I opened it. They asked me if I thought the virus was god's punishment for mankind's iniquities. I smiled and closed the door, leaving them standing on my front porch. I walked into the living room and tore a pillow in half.

I don't like it when people come to my house, except for the mail carrier and the deliverymen. I like to order things online. I collect blunt and edged weapons and have a large collection in our garage. Currently my obsession is hatchets, though I have swords, axes, spears, fighting sticks, and dozens of knives and daggers. The Nepalese kukri is a formidable weapon, if you've never seen one. I have two.

I went on Reddit this evening out of morbid curiosity and found a forum about serial killers. One user asked the question, "What is the most effective way to kill a person?" There were a lot of harsh jokes about the post but one guy gave an honest, insightful response. This is what he said:

"Yeah the best spots are the discos downtown where all the Molly kids hang out on Saturday nights. What yer lookin for is a young drunken female who's gotten separated from her friends, sloppy and streetwalkin and gettin lost down dark alleyways. These are the best ones to cuddle. Best to wear a longer coat to hide the what have you, and grubby clothes so you look like a bum, and just keep a low profile in yer parked car til the millennials spill out of the club at 2 AM. When you have yer target in yer sights, move swiftly and with purpose but don't act like it. Just amble on up to that hot pink dream and take out yer whacker, or you can beg her for change first if you like the interaction. The back of the head is best if you can manage it. Knock not once, not twice, but thrice, and she'll drop like a teenaged boy's balls. Oh, you'll also need some kind of blanket to cover her up while you go to work. Usually there's cardboard and dirty rags in the gutters if you forget to bring one. You probably won't be noticed cuz it's the city and the cops don't care and all the kids are stoned to the gills and pickled on alcohol. Now is when the fun begins. Don't fuck her like the perverts, but stop to admire her ruined husk in the streetlight before you begin. I like to say a prayer to the Blessed Virgin but that's just me. Take yer trusty slicer out of yer pocket and take whatever you want. It's like a shoppin spree. Some guys like to take the tits and put em in Mason jars. I know a guy who has shelves of em down in his basement. Me, I go for the baby makin parts. Nothin beats a good uterus, you just gotta know where to find it. The first few times will be like bobbin for apples but you'll get the hang of it. Keep practicin and you'll do just fine."

He didn't leave a name, but I found myself fascinated. His response seemed unbelievable though intriguing. I felt excited. I don't have a vehicle so the city wasn't an option for me, but there was always my neighborhood. No one knew me because I stayed indoors and never socialized, so I wouldn't be recognized, especially at night. I live in an upper middle class suburb, mostly full of white Christian Republicans, so you rarely see the cops. It's rare to see anyone on the streets at night, other than the occasional dog walker from time to time.

Tomorrow night I'm going out with dad's old hatchet. Wish me luck.

It was a bust. No one was outside. I walked the perimeter of the neighborhood with dad's hatchet in my black pea coat but no luck. This is probably a good thing. More time to plan things out. I don't care who it is but it's going to be somebody. I'm going to do more research today and observe the comings and goings of the neighbors. People don't walk alone at night anymore except for me. I used to be afraid of everything before I lost mom and dad. Now I'll be the one to fear.

The killer's response stirred something in me. It gave me a sense of purpose again. I've always had morbid interests, and my thoughts and fantasies have always been of a violent nature. I have urges. Beauty offends me. It needs to be extinguished. The cows mowing their lime green perfect lawns in the summers. I want to dig them up. And winter, the hideousness of the pristine white snow. I like it when it becomes gray and black and dirty. My thoughts are ugly. I want to cover myself with shit and smear myself across the springtime evenings.

It's morning and I'm making coffee. I wonder if you could kill a person with a spoon. It would probably take some effort, I imagine. The wind outside is howling like ten thousand wild animals and the air is cold. Memories of winter. More people will be outside as the temperature rises. Perhaps it would be best to enter a crowd and do it so no one would notice. Maybe with a garrote. Silent death. I need to do more research.

Maybe it's best not to go out to do it. Maybe I should make them come to me. The mail carrier comes every day but I need him to deliver my packages, so that's out. I could always hire a whore to come over but that's too risky. Maybe an amateur though. Some slut off Facebook or something. I still fantasize about my triumphant march through the neighborhood, sneaking up behind someone, and whack! But that is probably unrealistic.

It's a good thing I don't have friends because I might accidentally start talking about this in my excitement. I've found online groups in which they openly discuss the subject, and those have been very helpful, though I haven't interacted with any of the members. It's just too dangerous. People report everything these days, and any form of social media is being monitored by someone or something. I just gotta keep a low profile until my goal is reached.

I can't sleep. It's the second night in a row. I've been watching documentaries about killers and feeling half dead myself. I'm starting to think that I would be better suited to being an ambush predator. I could hide and lie in wait for someone to approach, then crack them over the head and take off. Just leave the body there to be discovered. It's a pity that I don't have a car, because doing this in the city would be ideal. In the suburbs you would have to dispose of the body somehow. There is always the river. It's not too far from my house. I could wrap them in tarps with weights attached and dump them in the water. Or just leave them on the banks for the rats to eat.

I went for a walk this afternoon. There were a few cattle milling about and I thought about them as not human, not even really animal. They were just "forms." Flesh and bone and blood powered by electricity. These weren't "people." They were just... there. I didn't relate to them in any way. I suppose I'm a narcissist with a superiority complex. I kept my head down as I walked, noticing the cracks in the sidewalk in need of repair. I patched potholes and sidewalks for the city when I was a teenager. The men I worked with were fat and lazy and I did all the work because my parents instilled in me a strong work ethic. Not like those bums. They were just collecting a paycheck. Makes me sick.

The kids walked home from school today. I could easily lure one or two into my house if I wanted, but it seems too easy. Plus it's stupid because I would surely get caught. Heads full of hair and bald faces, lugging packs of books on their young backs. I remember that time in my life. Still, tying them up in chairs and bludgeoning them does strike me as appealing. But no, I'll go after their parents. I don't like breeders. If I did do a kid it would be one of the 4 PM students. I was a good student in high school and never served a single detention.

My beard is getting long. Mom always told me to cut it but I look terrible clean-shaven. My hygiene has suffered. I brush my teeth in the morning and keep my bald head clipped but that's it. Every now and then I chew off my nails so I don't poke my eyes when putting in my contact lenses. I've never showered often, which used to drive Mom mad. When memories like these surface, I miss them both.

It's a sunny day today and the dogs and their walkers are out and about. I bought dog treats at the grocery store and handed two of them to the pair of Rottweilers that live in the neighborhood. I asked their owner if I could and they smiled and said yes but I said little else to them. I just wanted to make the dogs happy. When I have an encounter with a person I suffer severe anxiety which is why I don't often leave the house.

I ordered a Plumb hatchet off a vintage crafts website a couple weeks ago. I am very pleased with it. The mail carrier smiled and I nodded my head as she handed me the package. I'm terrible at small talk. I don't want to talk about the weather or the virus or the miserable state of the nation. I prefer to remain apolitical and areligious, and after 12 years of Catholic indoctrination, I certainly don't want to be bothered by bible thumpers who come to my door every Sunday afternoon. They're the ones that really deserve the righteous fury.

It's evening now. I'm resting. I've developed a severe backache as a side effect of medication, and it's only comfortable when I lay on the couch. I'm watching cartoons. I remember watching them every Sunday before Dad took me to church. That was the only thing I resented about my father. His Catholicism. I never took pity on the Christ; I always thought he was reckless and got himself killed when it could have easily been avoided. I did enjoy learning about the science of crucifixion in Catholic middle school though. I went through a torture phase as a youngster and tried to learn as many historical torture methods as I could. Thumb screws and Iron Maidens fascinated me, and I often imagined my classmates being boiled alive.

The morning sun shines through my bedroom window as I'm assaulted by another day. I weigh myself on the bathroom scale. 179.2 lbs. I've lost some weight in recent weeks. I brush my teeth and tongue, gagging on the brush. I get dressed and go downstairs. It's 9 AM. I make coffee. I check my messages and take a nicotine lozenge. Quitting smoking is one of the most difficult addictions to break. I'm a recovering alcoholic.

Cold turkey. No AA, no nothing. I go for a walk. The air is still chill but the sky is blue. Cars are pulling out of driveways driven by cattle late for work. Soon the trees will be budding. I notice something out of the corner of my eye. It is a dead raccoon, run over by a car. I approach it for further inspection and notice the eyes rolled back into the head, the fur matted with blood, the tire mark. The city workers will come to clean it up so that everything is picturesque again. The world could use more dead raccoons.

I walk over to the sewer grate to see if I can find anything interesting. Just a few cigarette butts and paper scraps. When I was a kid I used to turn over rocks to see all the bugs living underneath them. Every kid does this. The hidden world is fascinating and even magical to a young child. Sometimes I wish I could see the world through those young eyes again, but that will never be.

The wind is blowing cold and I don't have a hat on so I turn toward home. Nothing of interest along the way, just the empty houses and the tall oaks. I unlock the door and go inside to the warmth. I take my coat off and go down to the basement to my carving station. I sharpen my knife on the leather and continue to carve the wood spirit I've been working on. It reminds me of my father. He taught me how to do this. Bass wood is best for carving because it's soft and light. I'm still a beginner but I watch a lot of online video tutorials and there's Dad's old carving books. Carving allows me to focus and catch a break from the intrusive thoughts. I can carve out an eye or a mustache without once feeling the urge to harm others. It has become my therapy. A gift from my dad, gone two years.

Mom used to plant flowers in the yard around this time of year. She was a hard working woman who loved me very much. We butted heads a lot, mostly because I was lazy about doing household chores. I inherited my anxiety from her, and she struggled with it too. She and my dad both got sick at around the same time two years ago, and I watched them diminish until they were gone. It's painful to think about. The virus took many lives and is still spreading. I'm still relatively young and healthy so I don't have to worry too much just yet, but, as with all things, I too will someday pass and be forgotten.

My work was trashed by the heads of the local art college so I stopped drawing and painting. My parents always encouraged me and had great expectations of my future success. I was told

I would be famous one day by many professors. I never became a great artist. I don't know if I can even call myself an artist anymore. The only things I make are these little wooden sculptures anyone could make. I want to be famous. I don't want to pass and be forgotten like the dead raccoon in the street.

It's noon. I've forgotten what day it is. There is a knock at the door. I open it and a man in a suit is standing on the front porch. I look the man in the eye and ask what he wants.

"Excuse me sir, do you have time talk about the virus and its possible link to the end of days?"

My skin prickles and blood rushes to my face. Who does this man think he is, asking me this ridiculous question? I become psychotic with rage. I take the knife in my hand that I was using to carve wood and plunge it into the man's face.

I drag the body inside and haul it down the basement stairs, leaving a trail of red in my wake. It is difficult to maneuver down the stairs. In the basement, I strip the man of his blood-splattered suit, take my dad's old saw and remove the head, arms, and legs from the torso. It is gruesome work but I'm efficient. There's a gold ring on his left ring finger. Some lady will be missing her husband. I take his wallet out of his pocket and thumb through the cash. Three hundred dollars. I've never been a thief but he's dead now and he won't be missing it. I get heavy black garbage bags from the kitchen and fill six bags. I feel no emotion. I can't put them in the trash bin, so I'll walk them down to the river later tonight. If I do it at night no one will notice. This is going to work.

It's 3 AM and the bags have been sitting in the basement for over 12 hours. I carry them up the stairs one by one. They're not that heavy now that the pieces are separated. One piece per bag; the heaviest being the torso. I put them in dad's wheelbarrow and take them down to the riverbanks five blocks away. No one is awake at this time of night. I find large rocks along the river and place them in the bags. I throw the bags one by one into the river. I take the wheelbarrow back home and leave it sitting behind the house. I go inside and pass out on the couch.

Rays of sunlight burst through the blinds and shock me awake. I look down at my shirt and see dark red splotches. I see the mess on the floor. I'll have to clean the basement today but I finally accomplished something. I didn't even plan it. It just happened. I don't feel bad about this. That man should have never mentioned the word virus to me.

I feel calm after the thrill and terror. I cleaned the basement thoroughly with bleach, so I should be okay. A pack of squad cars hasn't shown up on my lawn and it's been over 12 hours, so everything should be fine. I feel a lingering sensation of shame because Mom and Dad would be horrified, but they're gone. It's just me and the thoughts. I can't control them. They intrude my mind with visions of death and decay and devastation and are constant. Killing that Christian pissant relieved a lot of the pressure. I just gotta go with my gut from now on.

Life is good. I read my books, carve wood, listen to the radio and podcasts. I've lost interest in famous serial killers. I'm not trying to emulate anyone. I'm just being myself now. I've discovered that I enjoy killing people. I have to be smart about it. I can't go about it in a haphazard way. It's really just a matter of opportunity. Luck was on my side the other day. The preacher knocked on the wrong door at the wrong time. I feel at peace now. Mom and Dad would still love me.

It's evening. I've had my steak and potatoes and am just relaxing watching *Ren & Stimpy*. My cell starts ringing. I never answer my phone and it's an unrecognized number anyway, but it distresses me. I've started to feel a little paranoid. I've been watching the windows moreso than usual, imagining the police pulling up and breaking into my house. These feelings will pass. They come in waves at unexpected times though. I really shouldn't worry. It's just the anxiety, Mom would say. It'll pass, she would tell me.

I couldn't sleep again. I was up all night watching old cartoon shows and pacing the floors. There was nothing I could do to stay focused; my hands were shaky from nerves so I couldn't carve. I felt sick to my stomach. My lower back and right shoulder severely ached. I'm doing better now but I still feel off; I can almost feel the black river calling me, reaching for my body with oily black tar hands. Hopefully the bags sank to the bottom. I'd like to go back and make sure they haven't washed up on the banks but I'm afraid of going back there.

My mood has become unstable again. My thoughts alternate between terror and elation. One minute I'm paralyzed with fear at the prospect of spending life in prison; the next, I'm giddy with manic, homicidal hysteria. I keep shifting and I'm starting to question which is the real me; the beloved son or the murderer. I suppose I've become both. Then there is a voice telling me to kill as much as I can before I get caught, which is inevitable. I'm bound to make a fatal mistake somewhere along the way if I am to continue like this. But taking a life is so intoxicating, and I fantasize about stabbing that filthy Christian again and again.

If I'm going to be a murderer, I can't look the part. I trimmed my beard this morning and did laundry, and I ordered some nondescript clothing online. Real killers don't look like rock stars. You don't want to attract attention to yourself at any time. So I've gone from looking like a wild, unkempt hermit to a respectable middle-aged civilian. I'll have to work on my social skills too. Charm goes a long way and if I'm going to lure anyone I'll have to appear friendly and non-threatening. Maybe I'll get to know the neighbors. I'll have to establish trust before I go to work.

Another day at home. No random phone calls or knocks at the door thankfully. Just peace and quiet. I spent the day writing and carving. Finished another wood spirit. Thinking of attempting a larger piece, of what I don't yet know. The day to day life of a killer is pretty mundane. Serial killer fans are always fascinated by "what makes them tick," but the truth is we're pretty boring people. Our actions are what define us. Our actions make us famous. I burned all my dark clothes in dad's old firepit out back. My shipment of pastel shirts and khakis should be arriving soon. Superheroes wear costumes but the bad guys wear a disguise; for the real bad guys, a bland, casual disguise. I'm becoming more and more comfortable in my new role. It gives life meaning.

I received my package of clothes today and tried on an outfit. I look like a harmless suburban husband in it. I think I'll go for a walk. It's 2 pm and winter's chill is still in the air so I dress in layers. I hide a ball peen hammer in my jacket and leave the house. The sun is out with wispy clouds painted across an endless sky. Signs of new life are beginning to emerge. Soon everything will be green. I walk a few blocks, past the high school and the cemetery. A lone man is walking several yards ahead of me. He looks to be about my age, maybe a little older. He's wearing a red baseball cap and an American flag sweatshirt. Patriotic filth. Or at least the wrong kind of patriotism. I hasten my steps while removing my hammer, get within striking distance, and crack him hard on the temple. He drops like a load of bricks. I take out my blade and stab him in the throat until he stops gasping. No one else is within view. The occasional car drives by but no one is paying attention. I stuff the body into a dense patch of bushes and continue my walk, dropping the knife into a sewer grate in the street. If you use knives, invest in cheap ones, and buy them in bulk if you can. If you use knives to kill they must be disposable.

I'm a bit shocked at how easy it is to kill a person and get away with it. People think the city is dangerous but no one suspects the suburbs. The cows wave and smile to each other every morning before work. They sit and drink beer together in the evenings. My only social interactions have been online, where I talk to my lady friends. I talked to Rose today. She's a waitress out in the cornfields of Iowa. A German blonde with blue eyes, a talented artist with a warrior spirit. We've been talking online for six years now. We tell each other everything and she has been a great source of support over the years, especially during the time of my parents' deaths. She has urges too, so we talk about that a lot. I told her what I had been up to lately and she urged me to exercise extreme caution, and I assured her that I do. She's the only woman I've ever loved aside from mother, and I would marry her if she didn't already have a boyfriend.

I can't sleep and my body is weak. I'm trying to keep my mind occupied with television. The news is all virus this, virus that, so I avoid it. I don't read the papers anymore. I don't want to be reminded. I remember when we were still together, our little family, we used to read and watch movies together. Mom and Dad would cook dinner. I don't remember much else. It's been two years. Occasionally I'll get a fleeting glimpse into my old life but those moments are becoming more and more rare. I don't feel pain, just happiness and gratitude to have had them in my life for as long as I did. When they became sick they were my top priority, but I have other priorities now.

I go online to do more shopping. I need more tools for work. I like to buy tools that can be used as weapons rather than actual weapons that are junk made in China. I want to build my collection so I'll have something for every occasion. There's a geologists' hammer on eBay that caught my eye. It should have the power to penetrate a skull and make a mess of the brain inside. I'm an artist again. I need a variety of brushes to paint my canvas red.

The ticking of the clock is the metronome to the music of my life. I watch as the hours pass by fully aware that I will pass someday too. I didn't catch the virus from my parents so I must have a strong immune system. I never become sick with colds or flus so I think I'm safe from it. The crisis is international in scope and we're two years in, and the cows keep dropping. When everyone is dying already, the killers have free reign.

When sleep finally came, my dreams were feverish with scenes of violence and war and plague. Screaming and gunshots and the ripping sound of a blade meeting flesh. I get out of bed and dress in my disguise. I haven't yet decided on my next woodcarving project. Maybe an animal this time. Life sized. I've always liked mountain lions. Sleek lone predators stalking the woods, my kind of animal. I go online to search for a photo reference. Yes, this one will do nicely. The photograph is of a screaming mountain lion, its fangs bared, its tongue red. Maybe I could do a bust of its head. It will be fun and it will kill time, and it would make Dad proud. I'll start work on it right away. But first I have to take care of some business.

I'm going out tonight. My first attempt at night walking was unsuccessful, but I'm hoping someone will be walking their dog late. I want to try it with Dad's Plumb hatchet again. It's sharp on one side, with a hammer on the back. It has good weight to it. It could easily split a skull wide open with a single blow to the back of the head. I don't know what to do about the dog if there is one. It would probably attack me and I'd have to kill it which I'd rather not do.

It's past midnight. I put on my black wool pea coat and hat, tuck the hatchet into the coat. I lock the door behind me and begin my walk. The sky is a murky dark gray, illuminated by streetlights. The streets are black like the river. It's still cold so I put my hands in my pockets and continue at a brisk pace. No one on my street. I turn the corner slowly and peer into the backyard of the house. There is a wooden deck with patio furniture and an old man with a white beard sitting and smoking a pipe. I inch my way along the side of the house, stopping to pick up a small rock. The old man continues smoking and doesn't notice anything. I step into the backyard and fling the rock into the bushes which catches the old man's attention. I rush him. In one fluid motion I remove the hatchet from my coat and swing it up and then down onto the old man's head, which collapses under the weight. There isn't much blood which surprises me. Just brain and skull mess. His body sinks further down into the chair. I don't stop to admire my work. I don't know who he was. He could have been someone's grandfather, father, or husband. Maybe he lived alone like me. Either way, he's dead now and I feel nothing. It was another accomplishment, nothing more.

I've begun roughing out the shape of the wooden mountain lion head. It's fun to use Dad's old carving tools, and he kept the garage stocked with bass wood for us to use. There's still a lot of it left in there. I like using my hands and fingers. I always had good manual dexterity, Dad would say. I've been thinking about last night. I'm a little bothered by the fact that I don't know who the old man was. Taking him out would have been so much more meaningful if I had known him as a man. He probably had the virus anyway though. I probably did him a favor.

I slept only for a few hours last night. The dreams are becoming more intense. Last night I dreamt that someone broke into my house and murdered me in my sleep. I still can't shake the feeling of dread it produced. The anxiety has lessened during the day; with each killing I feel more confident and powerful, but the dreams at night are terrible. I'm wondering if the insomnia is somehow subconsciously intentional, or if it's just a side effect of one of the drugs. Either way, I feel good about what I've been doing. I'm not going to stop because of a few bad dreams. I have to be dedicated and immerse myself in my craft.

3 PM on a Thursday and I'm hard at work on the mountain lion. Lots of people outside talking about the old man, whose body was discovered by his next door neighbor. The police have no suspects. He lived alone and there were no witnesses; still, they're interviewing anyone and everyone in the neighborhood. There was a knock at my door but I pretended I wasn't home. I don't have a car in the driveway. They must have bought it. I don't watch the news or read the papers but there've been a bunch of squad cars coming and going in a frenzy of flashing red and blue. Makes no difference to me. I didn't leave any evidence for them to trace. Kind of amused by how the neighborhood has become a circus. I guess that makes me the ringleader.

I'll have to wait for the circus to die down before I resume my task, which isn't a bad thing. It will give me time to collect more tools and work on the mountain lion. It's really starting to take shape. I was chipping away at the fangs earlier today. Such an intimidating animal. If it got your head in its mouth it could crush your skull. I've seen videos of people who have survived mountain lion attacks. They're few and far between because the animal almost always wins. I have become an animal, the apex predator of my neighborhood. It is my hunting ground, and I won't stop until they catch me. They never will.

I'm making coffee. I've been thinking about playing a game. Like leaving a calling card at the kill sites maybe, to mess with the police. I haven't decided on what it will be yet, but I'm beginning to enjoy the cat and mouse aspect of the detective and the killer. I always liked The Riddler from Batman, especially Frank Gorshin's performance of the character. The Riddler left clues for Batman, only they were riddles. The Riddler forced Batman to use his intellect to figure out the next crime. He wasn't some maniacal clown. He was an intellectual. I have my intellectual side and my animal side, like everyone, but in my case there's a more pronounced distinction. Which is the real me? I wonder. Is my core self the once beloved son who enjoys woodcarving and public radio? Or am I the cold, calculating killer that has taken over my persona?

When a reporter asks me someday, "Why did you kill all those people?" my response will be "Because they were there." I've always been a bit of a misanthrope, but I kill opportunistically.

I do it because I enjoy it. It's the same reason anyone does anything. It's passion. I wouldn't kill if it disgusted or morally offended me. I am amoral. Humans are no different to me than barnyard animals. "Why did the mountaineer climb the mountain?" Because it was there.

4:16 AM and I'm shaving my head. It's an irritating chore because you have to do it every other day to maintain the look. Some guys enjoy the process but I don't. I do enjoy having a smooth scalp. I hate the way I look with hair growth on the back and sides of my bald head. I have a small tuft of hair that grows right in front. When grown out, I look like a deranged cartoon clown. My goal is to look the least ridiculous as possible. I'm a serious person and I want to be taken seriously.

I wake at 8 AM. I don't know what to do with myself today. I don't work a job, due to disability, and my hobbies become tiresome after doing them all day every day. Maybe I'll just rest and listen to music. Yes, I will listen to *The Black Rider* by Tom Waits. It's been my favorite album since I discovered it in high school. Maybe I'll listen to that and try to paint. I'm a little sick of woodcarving at the moment. I must finish the mountain lion bust though. I have to keep myself occupied or

I will start having anxious thoughts. I can't go out on a walk right now. There is still a police presence in the neighborhood but with no evidence and no suspects they can't make an arrest. Tension is still high here though. People are wearing surgical masks when they go outside due to virus hysteria. It's been two years so the initial panic has been put on the back burner but people are still paranoid, and now there's a killer loose in the neighborhood. The poor cows are terrified. It's a gas!

I'm getting cabin fever. When a recluse gets cabin fever it's always bad. The local news media has picked up the story to spread further panic among the civilians, so now along with squad cars there are news vans and reporters and cameramen running everywhere outside my window. I'm not going outside. If I do I'll stay in my backyard. I don't need this nonsense. I know it will pass in a couple weeks but it's an annoyance. Had I known it would have stirred up this much chaos I might not have gone through with it. Yes I would have. I just have to be patient until everyone is once again distracted by the virus.

I need to be inspired. I should talk to Rose but she's at work right now. I took a shower this morning. I looked at myself at the mirror to see if my face had changed. I have a tattoo on my chest and arm. A Japanese dragon holding an apple. It was meant to be the serpent from the Garden, holding the apple to tempt me. I got it when I was 19, when I was still a good Catholic schoolboy. Even then I knew I was capable of destruction. I got the tattoo to remind me to keep up the struggle and not give in to the dark thoughts. How times have changed. I'm a different person now, and the tattoo has become irrelevant. I wish I could have it removed but I can't afford it. I look at the apple and wonder if things would have been different if Mom and Dad hadn't died. I wonder what they would think of me now. They were once so proud of me. I lived to please them. They are gone now, though, and I have taken a bite out of the apple.

I dropped out of college after a year and went on to work at a local tattoo parlour in the city. This was back when I had a car, an old jalopy I bought from my grandmother for 250 dollars. There was a guy there that had been a sniper for the Marines. He was a scary guy, covered in tattoos and facial piercings, a bad attitude. He was smart though. He murdered for a government check. I should have joined the military. Then I would have been recognized as a hero. The shop is gone. The owner, a fat Mexican man named Fred, died of diabetes.

A Sunday in mid March. Easter is coming up and the Catholics will be out in full force. There is a large gothic cathedral not far from my house where I was baptized and confirmed into the Catholic faith. Dad used to walk to it every Sunday morning when he was still able to walk. After high school I stopped going with him. I remember going to Mass and admiring the architecture, the stained glass windows, the statues of angels and saints. The cathedral was built by German immigrants sometime in the 19th century. It has aged well, though the congregation is now small and scant and mostly elderly. I used to have a classmate who called the place God's waiting room. I hate Catholicism now but I still love the old cathedral. It's the people inside it that offend me.

It's nighttime and I'm carving away at the mountain lion. I'm working on the eyes. The rest is complete. I chip away at the wood to define the contours of the eyelids, always keeping my blade sharp. Dad would have been so proud. I think I'll mount it in the living room when it's finished. We used to spend a lot of time in there watching TV and reading books. Dad would sit in his chair and read newspapers and economic magazines while Mom did the crossword puzzles. I would lay on the couch and text with my lady friends. I've always had a lot of female friends. I find their company more pleasant than that of men. They're better conversationalists. I just hate it when they tell me about their menstrual cycles. So far my kills have been three men. I wonder what it'd be like to kill a woman.

Mother was good to me. She was overprotective but I knew it was because she loved me. I was her only child. She would always drive me to doctor's appointments and pick up my medications from the pharmacy. She cooked dinner almost every night and sometimes she would make me an egg sandwich for lunch. She had been a schoolteacher and loved children. She had a tender heart for anyone in need, though she did have bad anxiety and some control issues. She was a perfectionist, especially when it came to the house, and was always cleaning. I hated doing chores and we would often butt heads because I was a lazy, selfish jerk. I keep the house clean and tidy now, as she would have wanted. We were very close.

It's 9 PM, I have to take a shit. I walk into our small bathroom and lift the lid. I squeeze my bowels and out it comes. Luckily toilet paper is available again. Two years ago the foolish cows were buying it all up in bulk like squirrels hoarding nuts for winter. Those were bad times. Some conspiracy nuts are still saying that the government created the virus but I pay them no mind. Sure it's corrupt but they're not trying to kill us off. They need good little consumers to buy their products made overseas. They need an uneducated public to elect their puppets of the one percent. This is why I don't follow politics anymore.

8 AM and I'm making fried potatoes and onions like my dad used to make. On Christmas morning he made Eggs Benedict every year, my favorite breakfast. I sit down and eat. The cops and reporters have left the neighborhood. That's something to be thankful for. They never did find the body of the second one, the red-blooded American patriot. I hid him pretty well. They'll find him eventually when the temperature rises and he starts to stink. Never found the bags in the river either. I'm doing well. I'm going to do a woman next but after Easter. Even butchers take breaks.

Easter Sunday morning. The herds are moving toward the cathedral to worship and give thanks to their cow god. I hate Easter. Even the word Easter is stolen from a pagan holiday, just like the eggs and the bunny rabbits. The whole religion is a rip off of more ancient heathen beliefs and practices. The idea of prayer offends me. If I was their god I would hate them for asking me for so much shit. And of course it's utter hypocrisy given the herd's politics. If a black homeless man wandered into our neighborhood he would be arrested and removed immediately, yet I've murdered three people and am listening to Kurt Cobain, comfortable in my home.

Had a corned beef sandwich on rye for lunch, now I'm putting the finishing touches on the mountain lion, the fine detail work. I carve out little lines for the fur on the neck. It's an exercise in patience, which is something I need to work on. Those first few kills were pretty sloppy, especially the first two. The old man with the pipe got the finesse treatment. I want to have finesse and precision, like the mountain lion. If I'm going to take out a woman next I'm going to need it. It's warmer outside now and the ladies of the neighborhood have started jogging again. I don't want to run after them so I'm either going to have to ambush or use a projectile. I like my hatchet. Maybe I could order some throwing axes and practice with those in the backyard.

I've finished the mountain lion bust and am very proud of how it looks. The way the eyes squint at the opening of the fanged jaws, the musculature of the neck, the erect tongue. Dad would be proud of me, maybe Mom too. She was always hesitant to praise my work. That's just how she was. The important thing is that I'm proud of myself. I completed a challenging task. I accomplished something. There will be more accomplishments to come.

10 PM. I'm online and shopping and talking to Rose. I told her about the throwing axe idea and she became very excited. She loves weapons, especially guns. I've never liked guns so I don't use them in my work. I always thought that they were a coward's weapon, because you don't own the death, you don't see and feel the life draining from the body like you did in the old days on the battlefield. You're too removed. No intimacy. I take my work very personally because I enjoy it so much. I'm starting to think that even throwing axes would take some of the pleasure out of it. Rose doesn't think so. They're going to be jogging though and I'm not about to go chasing a woman down the street with a hatchet in my hand. Maybe Rose is right. She's happy that I'm doing something productive again.

Rose hates her job and is jealous of me because I don't have to work a 9-5 like everyone else. We kid about it. She says she's a slave for tips from cheap, fat, ugly, disgusting trolls. We have the same outlook. We send each other gifts sometimes: Christmas, birthdays. She sent me a Viking drinking horn once and even etched a rose into it for me. I don't drink anymore but it was still very touching. We joke about getting married in Hell because surely that's what awaits us so I secretly hope there is a Hell even though my common sense doesn't allow me to believe in an afterlife. We love each other in the same way I loved my parents.

Easter was early this year and now it's April Fools' Day. I can't decide what to do but I want it to be violent. I ended up ordering the throwing axes but they haven't arrived yet so I'll have to use one of my other tools. The Plumb always gets the job done so I'll have to find a walker. Those jogging cows move too fast, and are fit. If I botch it up I'd probably get my ass kicked and arrested. You can't be too careful. Still, after creating beauty out of the wood with the mountain lion bust, I now want to destroy something beautiful. I'll just dick around til nightfall and then go out to see what I can find out on those black streets.

11:36 PM. It's late and the cows have stopped driving their cow cars. I'm sitting in my dad's chair looking out the window. Every now and then I see a jogger. Time to put my coat on, I think. I go down the basement and retrieve the hatchet, go back up the stairs and out the front door, locking it behind me. It's a Sunday night so there isn't much happening; everyone is indoors on social media posting selfies and recipes and memes and political rants. But there are the occasional runners and walkers, joggers in their brightly colored costumes. Makes for an easy target. We have several big oak trees in our front yard surrounded by bushes. I used to hide in them when Dad and I would play hide and seek when I was little. I crouch down in the bushes with the hatchet and wait.

Fifteen minutes pass and I'm trying to remain as silent as possible. Then she comes into view. A lone female in neon orange jogs toward the front of the house. I get my hatchet ready. The timing will be everything. Just as she's about to pass the bushes I spring forward and dash toward her, hatchet high above my head, holding it in a fist. I come within striking distance and before she has a chance to scream I bring down the hatchet on top of her pretty blonde head. She drops dead at my feet. No one around to witness it. I pick her up, cradling her in my arms as if she was Rose, and take her back to my house. I take her down the basement, strip her of the neon orange, and turn her into six big chunks like I did the preacher. She has a beautiful floral tattoo on her right arm. I stop for a moment to admire it, then put each chunk into a black, heavy duty garbage bag and carry the bagged pieces of her body up the stairs and out the door and to the river. The process is becoming easier. I dump the bags on the riverbanks and walk home.

The next morning, I'm eating a bowl of bran flakes and thinking about last night. She was the first woman I've killed. I feel bad about it. That could have been Rose. Certainly it was someone's "Rose." I hope she wasn't someone's mother. It was hard to tell at night but she looked to be in her early 30's so it's entirely possible. Maybe I should stick to men. I need to stop thinking so much. I had a writing professor once who told the class that "Thinking is for morons." Thought gets in the way of action, and I should be focusing on my next project instead. If I sit around and brood over all this I'll drive myself mad. I have to be a mountain lion, an apex predator. Predators don't discriminate.

1:17 PM. Wednesday. The throwing axes came in the mail today. I decided to practice being friendly so I said hello to the mailman and we talked a little bit. His name is Al and he's 35, a few years younger than me. He joked about all the packages he's been delivering to my house lately. I chuckled and said it was all equipment for my work, and that I worked from home. He laughed and said he wished he could work from home instead of pounding the pavement all day every day. "Good exercise," I said and winked. We fistbumped and he went on his way. It felt good to talk to a person face to face again.

I take the two axes out of the packaging and inspect them thoroughly. They're sharp and well-balanced. They have a good weight and feel to them. I go outside through the back door and into the yard, heading for the garage. I think Dad had some black spraypaint left over from an old project. I know we have plywood boards. Yep, I was right on both counts. I take a sheet of plywood and lean it against the back fence, shrouded in tall privacy bushes, and take the paint can and spray a black target onto the wood. With an axe in each hand I walk about ten yards away from the target. The neighbors can't see me through the tall bushes, so I need not worry. My first attempt misses the board entirely and hits the fence. This is going to take patience. I throw maybe 150 more times until I can hit the outer edge of the target. I'm pleased with my progress. I think I have a knack for it.

The day I have dreaded all week has finally come: Cleaning Day. I hate doing it but Mom always liked a clean house. I tore up all the carpeting and threw out all the rugs after Mom and Dad died because vacuuming is something I loathe, so it's all hardwood flooring which is easy to clean. I dust, I do the dishes, clean the kitchen counters, I scrub the floor. I clean the toilet, scrubbing the piss and shit off the inside and outside of the bowl. I don't bother with the upstairs because it's just the two bedrooms and I allow myself to have a messy room. I thrive in chaos and squalor. I do appreciate the method behind cleaning; scrubbing a floor or a toilet is much like cleaning up body mess, which I enjoy. After several hours of labor I sit down on the couch and have an NA beer, thinking about Rose, and the mailman, and Mom and Dad. The people I care about. To hell with all the rest.

The next morning I wake early and go through my usual routine. I'm showering more often now and keeping a neat appearance so as not to attract attention. I make sure to wash my hands thoroughly because that's what you do in Viral World. I'm not shaving my beard to wear a surgical mask though. That's ridiculous, and I never go anywhere except for the grocery store and pharmacy. I throw some axes around 10 AM. I'm getting better. I can almost hit the target from 15 yards away, and when I use them for work the targets will be much closer, but they'll be moving. I'm not worried. I'll practice on the squirrels.

At noon I eat French onion soup and wait for the mail. I'm really just waiting to talk to Al, or Saint Nick as I have decided to call him, because he comes bearing gifts. I think I'll make another online purchase just so I can feel the anticipation again. Then Saint Nick will come and bring it to me and we can talk. About an hour later he shows up and stuffs the junk through the slot in the door. He struggles with it a bit so I open the door and we exchange pleasantries. It turns out that Saint Nick is a family man; he has a wife and two little girls. Hearing that makes me happy. I don't know why. I guess I'm happy for Saint Nick and his little family. This is unusual for me.

4 PM and I need a drug refill. Mom used to take me to my appointments but when she died the doctor agreed to do the sessions by phone. I talked to him the other day and told him that my mood swings are bad right now, that the anxiety has become crippling. I don't even want to walk to the pharmacy and be out in public but I need the Lithium. I put on my pea coat but only carry a legal 3 inch blade in my pocket. I begin my walk. The pharmacy is only a half mile from my house, next to the grocery store. The air is still chilly but signs of life are beginning to emerge. There are green buds on the oak trees, once black and bent like old, arthritic hands. I don't

encounter anyone on my walk. Most people are still self-isolating and working from home due to the virus. Even Saint Nick expressed concern for his little girls during our chat, how their school is closed until further notice. I hope they'll be okay.

I reach the pharmacy and open the door, spraying hand sanitizer on my hand after touching the handle. Everyone carries sanitizer these days. Luckily there are only a few customers so I make my way to the counter without my anxiety flaring up. I hand the pharmacist the empty bottle with the refill printed on the label and she tells me it will be fifteen minutes. I walk over to the greeting card aisle and look for a card to send to Rose. I can't find anything disgusting or deviant so I give up. Just cards with cats and condolences. When my name is called over the speaker I walk back to the pharmacy register. I pay with my debit card and take the bag. The refill will last a few weeks. I leave the pharmacy, dousing my hands in sanitizer, and walk home.

On the walk home there were a couple dog walkers but most people are staying inside. Funny how everyone has become a hermit like me. I enter my house. It smells like Mom and Dad, or maybe it's just my imagination playing tricks on me. I still feel their presence from time to time. I know they're gone. It's just my own sentimental feelings. I take the bottle of Lithium out of the paper bag and open it, and pop a capsule along with the rest of my afternoon psychotropic salad. The pills are all different shapes, sizes, and colors, kinda festive. Later, I go into the backyard and throw my axes until dusk.

10 PM, it's raining. I coated the mountain lion bust in beeswax and mounted it above the mantle of the fireplace. I'm lying on the couch sucking a nicotine lozenge and listening to Nick Cave's *Murder Ballads*, one of my favorite albums. I oil my axes and sharpen them and think about my next task. It would be risky and difficult but I've been thinking about taking out a couple. I see them now, walking down the street holding hands, happily in love. I've never been one for romance. Anything sexual disgusts me. I don't understand why people love pornography so much. I just laugh at it and feel sick afterwards. Maybe if it was artfully filmed it might be interesting to me. But watching cows fucking and all the bodily fluids makes me ill. I think I'll do a couple next. I've gotten pretty good with the throwing axes and am eager to test them out. I'll have to take a knife to finish the job but that's no big deal. I'll have to wait for the rain to stop though. It'll give me more time to practice.

The rains haven't let up, the sky is gun metal gray. I've had my eggs and fried potatoes, my psychotropic salad, my coffee and lozenge. I hate rain. I don't like being wet, which is probably why I don't like bathing. I don't like the snow much either, because you have to shovel it. But I enjoy being cold. In high school I took ice cold showers to build up my endurance to pain. I was into self-mortification back then and wanted to join a monastery. I am a monk now in this empty house. A warrior monk. I fight with my mind every day and night like some Viking berserker on an ancient battlefield. I kill to externalize the thoughts, to get them out of my body. A ruined corpse is a work of art. I am an artist.

3:30 PM. Almost time to eat another salad. I didn't lie to the doctor; I have been more moody lately and the anxiety has been bad again. I just declined to tell him the reasons why. It's been raining all day and I'm stuck inside, not that I mind it. I'm just feeling lonely. Rose is at work and Saint Nick hasn't showed up yet, and when he comes I don't want to make him stand in the rain while we talk. I should do some shopping. I need a balaclava for my next task. Taking out two people at once is going to be very difficult. I need to work out the logistics before going to work.

On the computer I order a balaclava and some other supplies; some black leather gloves, a new knife. I decided to be patriotic and buy American so I ordered a Buck knife to finish the job. Rose signs on and I say hello. We bullshit with each other for about an hour. She's tired of her boyfriend playing computer games all the time. When I tell her about my next big hit she becomes excited. She's very enthusiastic about everything which is one of the reasons I like her so much. She says hardly anyone comes to the diner anymore because of the virus. She's looking to get into a new line of work. I suggest that she become The Cornfield Killer and she cracks up. I'm lucky to have her in my life.

When you're unemployed and live alone you never know what day it is. If it weren't for my phone to tell me, it would be one very long weekend. Now that the schools are closed I can't tell whether it's a weekend or a weekday. There are no students walking home anymore. Everything is on lockdown. They shut down the bars and restaurants. Luckily they kept the grocery stores open so the cows can get their feed. People don't go outside much. Every now and then I'll see a dog walker with an umbrella. Poor bastards. They'd make good target practice to prepare me for the big hit.

9:34 PM and I'm feeling the itch. I've been watching the dogwalkers for the last two hours. There aren't many but it's better that way. The rain has let up so everything outside is dark and wet and smells like worms. I put on my coat and hat, grab my axes, go outside and hide in the bushes down the street. I should really invest in a Ghillie suit so I'll disappear better into the brush. Black clothes will do for now. A walker without a dog approaches. I get ready. As soon as they're within a few yards I rise from the bushes and chuck an axe at their body. It twirls through the air and strikes their chest, burying itself deep in the lungs. I pounce on the walker, remove the knife from my pocket, and slit their throat. Their eyes roll back into their head like a dead raccoon. It's another woman, obese, middle-aged. Too heavy to carry so I haul the body into the street hoping a car will run it over. I take my knife and carve a cross into her forehead to throw the cops off.

Later that night I'm startled by sirens and flashing red and blue lights. It's raining again. The cops are out in full force and the media just showed up. This is the second murder discovered in the neighborhood in the past month. Too bad they don't know about the other three. I stay inside. There's a knock at the door. Two police detectives, one thin, one fat. They question me asking if I'd seen anything unusual in the last few hours. I tell them that I've been down in my basement carving wood. I had changed back into my casual costume after returning home. My yellow polo shirt and groomed beard didn't give the cops any reason to doubt me. They tell me to stay indoors and that this will all blow over soon, and to have a good rest of the evening. I tell them good luck in their investigation and close the front door, making sure it's locked. That was close.

The next morning the cops are back with the media and they're interviewing everybody. When Saint Nick comes to the door to drop off my packages we talk about it and he tells me that the murders are all over the news. He says they're calling him The Hatchet Man. I'm not interested, I tell him. What a stupid name for a killer. I change the subject and ask Saint Nick what music he listens to. He tells me that he's in a punk rock band called Online Concubine and that they used to play shows all over the Midwest until the virus cancelled all their shows and tours. I ask to buy a CD and he says he'll bring it tomorrow with enthusiasm in his eyes. I'm happy and excited to listen to it.

I walk to the couch and sit down with my packages. I remove the cheap knife from my pocket and slit the tape on the boxes, and open them with pleasure. The camo makes me look like a forest ninja. The black leather gloves fit well too. And the Buck knife is beautiful. Brass and wooden handle with a 3.75 inch lockback blade. I always say stock up on cheap knives but I wanted to treat myself to something nice as a reward for completing the mountain lion bust. And for my other recent accomplishments too.

I decide to take a bath. It will soothe and comfort me after all the chaos on the streets. I'm going to have to hold off on the big hit because there's a couple squad cars parked down the street keeping an eye on things. It makes me uncomfortable, trapped in the house and under surveillance. I might have to expand my territory to avoid getting caught. If I ever get caught I'll be famous, but not for my art like I wanted. But for something bigger than art. I'll become notorious. I could be like The Riddler. Maybe they could call me The Ringleader, since I've become the leader of this media circus. I'll have to think more on it. I want a really good killer name.

It's late. 2 AM according to my cell. The bars would be closing now if the bars were open. I'm lying in bed unable to sleep. I pull away the covers and get up, wearing only socks and briefs. It's a little chilly so I put on my robe and go downstairs. I pop a lozenge and sit down on the couch and turn on the TV. More virus panic, the wars, though I did make local news. The reporter has little information to give other than the names of the victims and where the bodies were found. Police think the killer could be religiously motivated because of the cross carved into the female victim's forehead, but other than that, nothing. They have no suspects and no evidence of anything other than the bodies. They do know that some kind of axe was used in both slayings so they've dubbed the killer "The Hatchet Man." Still sounds dumb to me but it'll do for now. One day I'll have a great name. The moo cows will write books about me.

9 AM. I have to go buy groceries again. Hopefully they've restocked the shelves. Steaks, eggs, bread, milk, onions, potatoes, ginger beer and NA beer. That's what I'm after. I put my casual Friday clothes on and head out.

The rains have stopped, but people are still indoors in full panic mode. It's becoming rare to see anyone walking down the street these days. All the cows have withered hands from washing them so much. I wash mine too but I don't go overboard with it. I reach the store and step inside in a nonchalant manner and put my new gloves on before touching the shopping cart. I push the cart down the aisles until I've found everything I need, then I make my way to the self-check out. Not many people in the store today at this hour so I avoid interaction entirely which pleases me. I punch the buttons with gloved fingers and put the groceries in plastic bags. I pay with my debit card, take my groceries, and leave the store out into the rain.

I'm sopping wet when I get home. Time to change out of these clothes and put the groceries away. I pop a lozenge. I decide to just wear my robe since I'm not going anywhere else today. I wash my hands before touching the grocery bags. After everything is in its place I go over to the couch and sit down. I have a few DVD's of my favorite movies. I put Brazil on. It's my favorite. I love dystopian films even more now that the world is a viral dystopia. It's like watching the news only I'm not in it. I look up from the TV to admire my mountain lion. Fierce. I don't like domestic cats but I love big wild cats. I love how they're so deadly and efficient. I look up to them. I hope to one day be as cunning and effective as the mountain lion.

4 PM. Time for psychotropic salad. I take two pills in the afternoon and take a total of ten every day. I called Dr. Berekin today to tell him I'm doing better. My moods have

stabilized and the anxiety has reduced. I'm usually pretty even keel in the springtime. This doctor is a good man. He has a wife and two children. A family man. I'll never be a family man. My parents were my family. I'm a solitary lion now planning my next kill. I'll have to hit another neighborhood. I like how the media played up the cross. They probably think the killer is an Islamic terrorist. That's good news for me. Maybe they'll call me the Ash Wednesday Killer next.

I watch the 6 o'clock local news. Mostly virus stuff, but there is a report on what they're now calling "The Ash Wednesday Killer." Called it. A body was discovered in some bushes, not far from the other two crime scenes. It was badly decomposed, but police were able to identify the man after finding his wallet and ID. Some jackass Trumper. I'm glad I took him out. I hate those people. The reporter says that the victim had been struck in the head with a blunt object, and stabbed repeatedly in the throat. No sign of the killer was found. No cross on the victim's forehead. Still, the reporter said, the murder occurred within the immediate vicinity of two other recent homicides, so it's likely that there is a connection, authorities are saying. I turn the TV off.

I sleep fitfully and wake at dawn the next day. I'm eager to talk to Saint Nick. Hopefully he'll have his CD for me. He won't be here til afternoon, so I'll have to keep myself occupied until then.

3 PM. Saint Nick has come bearing gifts. I open the door and greet him. He's balding and has a beard like me, except he's leaner and more fit from walking all day every day. He asks me if I've heard about the Ash Wednesday Killer. I say that I saw a news report last night. Saint Nick lives not far from my neighborhood and he has concerns for himself and his family. Being a mail carrier is dangerous, he says. He'd be an easy target, he says. I reassure him that he and his family will be fine so long as they keep their hands washed. We both laugh. He hands me the CD and I thank him. I look at the cover and it's a drawing of a diseased baby. Let me know what you think, he says. I promise him that I will.

Saint Nick's band is great! Online Concubine reminds me of gritty street punk I listened to in college, like The Beltones. Nick is vocals and lead guitar, very talented. Great gruff voice and catchy riffs. I like it a lot. Looking forward to telling him that when I see him again tomorrow. Right now I'm sitting in Dad's chair sucking a lozenge, looking out the big window. It's

5 PM but everyone works at home now so there aren't many cars on the street. I'm taking a little break from hunting until Ash Wednesday Killer mania dies down. I haven't carved anything since the lion head; I really should get back to work down there. I practice axe throwing a few times a week. I think I could be a champion in one of those novelty axe throwing bars, but those are all closed now.

I'll have to find a new hobby until this all blows over. Maybe I could start a taxidermy collection. If I stay busy and focused on something the bad thoughts won't build up and send me spiraling into another episode. I can't afford to go back to the hospital. It would kill me this time.

11 AM. Another day, another dollar. Saint Nick will be here in a couple hours so I've got time to kill. I've already had breakfast and done all the dishes, so I can relax for now. I pick up my old, dusty copy of Mary Shelley's *Frankenstein* and read a few lines. I can't pay attention, my anxiety is acting up. I have to be more careful. It was foolish to leave that woman's body in the street. I have to dispose of the bodies like I did originally; at night, deep in the black river. I can't be seen dragging bodies around though. I wish I could afford a car; a pickup would be best. But I'm living government check to

government check, and I can't afford to make so grand a purchase, even if it was a used vehicle. I'm not taking any more chances, certainly not on a used truck that could break down at any time. I'll have to start saving.

1:30 PM. When I hear a knock at the front door, I open it to find Saint Nick standing on the porch waiting to hand me my mail. His first question is "How did you like it?" I tell him how I loved the album and congratulate him on creating such a wonderful piece of music. He's overjoyed. We talk music for a few minutes and I recommend that he check out The Beltones and his eyes grow wide with excitement. I like Saint Nick. He's a good guy. Sometimes I wish I could be more like him

I spend the rest of the afternoon throwing axes out in the backyard until the sun begins to set. I've hit the bull's eye more than a few times. I'm happy with my progress. I set the axes down on Dad's work bench in the garage, and sit in a wooden rocking chair next to the back door of the house. I pop a nicotine lozenge and play with it in my mouth. I'll probably be sucking on these damned things for the rest of my life. I'm a hopeless addict. But at least I was able to give up the booze. The doctor told me I couldn't drink anymore because alcohol interacts with the medications. I complied and said goodbye to the bar forever. I miss it but it's closed down now due to the virus. It's down to grocery stores and pharmacies and those are the only places I go anyway so my life hasn't been affected much. Unless you count Mom and Dad.

I go inside and grill up a steak. I eat and clean up the mess. I sit on the couch and space out for a few hours, lost in thought. I look up at the mountain lion head and am reminded of my task. I'm not going to carve any more crosses or leave any kind of calling card because it will only increase my chances of getting arrested and be given a stupid killer name by the press.

11:35 PM. I make my attempt at sleep. I put on my robe and go back downstairs. I'm feeling agitated even though I have no reason to be. I must be having a mild episode. I ate my psychotropic salad before going to bed so I should be alright. But I don't feel alright. Maybe the house is getting to me. What was once friendly and familiar now seems hostile and foreign. I've been here too long but I have nowhere else to go. My government check won't allow me to relocate. I can't even afford a decent car. Where would I go? I've always wanted to live in Norway. I love Norse mythology and Vikings and its humane healthcare system. But all the borders have been closed since the outbreak, and the global economy has tanked. I know a little bit about the outside world but not much.

I passed out on the couch at 2 AM and managed to sleep til 7 AM. No bad dreams. No dreams that I can remember at least. I eat potatoes and onions and go online. No one is signed on at this early hour, not even Rose. I feel alone so I decide to do some retail therapy. I browse the axes on eBay. A fireman's axe would be nice to have. What I really need is a Ghillie suit. I hop on over to their website and browse their selection. I can get a good one for under 100 dollars. That's within my budget for the month. It'll make me look like Swamp Thing and I'll blend into the bushes perfectly. I place my order. This will give me something to look forward to in the mail. It should arrive in a couple weeks. I won't be able to walk down the street wearing it so I'll have to transport it in a bag and change into it in my killing den, then back out after the job is complete. I can't wait for Saint Nick to bring it to my door.

Dreary afternoon but no rain. The misery sky hangs heavy as if in mourning for the lives lost to the virus. I'm in the basement carving a Santa Claus figurine to give to Saint Nick. It's an easy job, takes me a couple hours to complete it. He'll love it. The cows would say I am being thoughtful. I just want to do something nice for a change, and Nick let me listen to his CD, and he brings me my packages, so it's just a small token of my gratitude. I'm listening to *Wish* by The Cure. Haven't listened to it since high school. Back then they were my favorite band and I still love them. "Friday, I'm In Love" always cheers me up, but my favorite track is "To Wish Impossible Things." It hits me deep.

1:45 PM. There is a familiar knock at the door. It's Saint Nick, the man himself. He hands me my usual junk mail and we talk a little bit. When I give him the Santa Claus figurine, he loves it. He doesn't stop thanking me and tells me I'm very talented. I ask about his family and he says they're doing fine but that they're confined to the house. I ask how he's holding up and he says that he's not dead yet. We laugh. I tell him that I have a big package coming and he becomes excited with curiosity. I don't tell him what it is, just that it's for work. We elbow bump and say "Tomorrow. Same bat time. Same bat channel." He steps off the porch and makes his way to the next house.

I sort through the garbage mail. Mostly ads and clothing catalogues for my mom. Dad's fly fishing and cigar catalogues. Another disability renewal form that I have to fill out. I get them every few months. The government wants to know if I'm still disabled and unable to work, but they're really just trying to cut costs on disabled people and save money. My condition is permanent I always tell them. I've worked jobs in the past until the episodes and anxiety got out of hand. That was when I moved back home with mom and dad, because I have great difficulty with simple tasks, like cleaning or operating a cash register. The sniper tattooist once told me that I was both the smartest and stupidest person he had ever met and that stuck with me. I'm rather inept socially, but it's only due to lack of practice. I hate the cows so why bother. It's so rare for me to meet a genuine human, like Rose or Saint Nick, or my parents. I'm not going to search them out. Besides, I have work to do.

I throw axes in the backyard for a few hours, then go inside and research axe fighting techniques. I want to become an expert with my tools. I read about this while chatting with Rose. She's at home due to the virus. She doesn't know when they'll reopen the diner so she's been searching for jobs online. We mostly talk about that. Her boyfriend is in computers and they're living off his income for the time being. She feels guilty but there's nothing she can do about it. I tell her that I've been feeling lonely and she tells me to stay busy and that she loves me, which I know she does. I order a kukri dagger and have it shipped to her house. She loves kukris.

Five cows down. Three men, two women. I don't know what number I'm shooting for; I don't need to break any records. I'm not in competition with those other deranged slobs. It's been a while since my last hit. I'm going to wait for my suit to arrive before I go at it again. I could use a break anyway. I enjoy the urges and the relief that comes with every kill, but it takes its toll mentally, emotionally, and physically. I am getting in better shape from walking so much and throwing axes out back. I should exercise more but I'm lazy. If I did it would be for work and not vanity, so maybe that would motivate me. Maybe I'll order some weights online later tonight.

Ash Wednesday Killer Mania has died down since there haven't been any recent killings. I watch the news and they say that police suspect it to be the work of someone from the city. Certainly it wasn't a white suburbanite, I chuckle to myself. I guess white privilege includes murder. Fucking racists. I grill a steak, eat, shit, and go back to the couch. I can't decipher my mood. I know I'm not depressed; common unhappiness, maybe, but not hysterical misery. The urges are getting stronger. The doctor will want to increase the antipsychotic. I don't think I'll take it. I enjoy the urges and the work that I do. They're going to make me famous one day, if I ever get caught.

I'll have to just keep at it; keep piling dead cows onto the body count meter.

8 PM. I'm feeling the old itch again. I can't wait another week for the Ghillie suit. I'll just have to wear my usual get up, my black pea coat and hat. I'm going down by the river this time. Maybe there'll be an adventurous walker down that way, which would be great for me because then I wouldn't have to haul their body around. Haven't used the Plumb in a good while. It needs sharpening, so I sharpen it with the file and leather. I'll wait a couple more hours before I head out. It's Saturday, I think, so there will be more people out and about. I'm excited. I read *Heavy Metal* to pass the time.

10:15 PM. I put on my coat and hat, pick up the hatchet, and leave the house. I keep my coat buttoned with the Plumb tucked inside, and make my way down to the river. I walk the banks avoiding branches and big rocks. I'm just a normal guy going for a riverside walk on a Saturday night. I walk about a quarter mile along the riverbank until I happen upon a man fishing the river. Memories of Dad hit me for a brief moment, but I clear them from my mind. I walk up to the man and ask if he's caught anything. Not tonight, he says. I stand next to him for a few minutes, watching his line in the water. There's a tug. The man jerks the rod up and begins reeling. Now is the moment, while he's not paying attention to me. I take out the Plumb and strike him in the head. He drops the fishing pole and falls to the ground, but he's not dead yet. You cocksucking motherfucker! he yells at me. I can see the red crack in his head. I didn't hit him hard enough. I take the hatchet and proceed to make a mess of his head until it's all brains and fragments of bone and blood on the banks. I clean my hatchet in the river, leaving the body on the banks. No one else is in sight in any direction. I race back to the house.

I open the back door and go inside. I'm shaken. It wasn't supposed to be like that. Sloppy. They're going to find that body and it will be a circus again. I'll be questioned again. It's hard keeping up appearances. At least I tried a new approach. I didn't ambush him like the others; I engaged him in conversation first. I don't know how he survived that first blow. Maybe my hatchet skills have gotten rusty. Or maybe I'm getting weak. I really ought to order those weights soon.

It's 11:45 and I'm blasting Nirvana's *Bleach* throughout the house. I feel drunk from the kill, sloppy as it was. Smashing that guys brains to pulp, even though it wasn't part of the plan, was a pleasure and a delight. I go online. Rose is on and so I tell her what just happened. Gotta cull the herd one way or another, she says. She goes on to thank me profusely for the kukri. She says she chopped a coconut in half with it. Rose is not a murderer, though she could be. She has the mindset for it. We realized that about each other early on, and that knowledge between us created a special kind of intimacy we've shared for six years. Now that she's off work we have more time to talk. Talking to her helps repair the damage.

3 AM. I can't sleep. My mind is racing. This last kill could get me caught. My footprints are in the mud. I failed to think about that. I'll get rid of these boots and order new ones with a different tread pattern, just in case. I don't mind paying extra for overnight shipping. I go back online and order a pair of black leather Carolina combat boots. I feel better. I pass out on the couch.

8 AM. I cook eggs for breakfast. I need to get some fruit next time I go shopping. I like bananas. Maybe I'll get some sausage too. I have a few days before I'll have to go back out. Today I'm just relaxing, after the events of last night. I better not throw any axes today. I could carve, or write, or read. Or think. Maybe I'll dust off the old kukri next time, to throw the cops off. I'm pretty good with it and it's very effective. No

blunders like last time. If Rose can chop a coconut with it in one stroke then I could easily split a skull wide open.

At 2 PM I hear a friendly knock at the front door. I open it and am greeted by good Saint Nicholas, bearing gifts. My new issue of *Heavy Metal*, some more catalogues, some bills. Nick tells me that he's still afraid with the killer on the loose. I do my best to reassure him. We don't talk about the virus, but he tells me that his daughters are doing well but are driving their mother crazy being home all day. We laugh. I tell him that a package will be coming for me tomorrow and he becomes excited. For work? he says. Nah just some personal shit, I tell him.

What to do today? The house is still relatively clean. The dishes are done and the kitchen isn't a mess. Trying to keep things tidy for you, Mom. I pause for a moment and think of her and Dad and how they cared for me when I wasn't well. If they were still around I probably wouldn't be doing what I'm doing, so part of me is glad that it's just me now, so I can pursue my interests freely. I can finally express my thoughts and act on the urges I've been suppressing my whole life. I feel liberated. Perhaps the killer is my true self. Maybe I am more animal than man. I stare at the mountain lion on the mantle, the mountain lion head that I carved. I feel the power welling up inside my heart.

I'm on the couch staring at the wall. I like how it changes colors in natural light and artificial light. I take the new issue of *Heavy Metal* out of its plastic and leaf through it. I don't have the patience to read any of the stories right now though, so I just look at the illustrations. Robots and zombies and space warriors. I like that kind of stuff. When I was young I wanted to draw and write comic books when I grew up. When I got to art school I learned that dreams make no promises.

So I'm making new dreams and making them reality. I'm on the news. People fear me. I will slaughter the cows. Time for the old guard to step aside and give free reign to the new generation. A godless generation. A generation free of racism, sexism, and all other forms of bigotry. This is my time to shine in the light of the furious sun. No more hiding in the shadows. I will be famous one day. Books will be written about me. I will be worshipped as a fallen angel, betrayed by both god and man. This is my goal. This is my triumph.

I snap out of it. Calm down, I tell myself. It's time to take your pills. Just relax. I can't go off all half-cocked about this. I have to be professional. Don't let the thoughts take over. Every time you do you end up in the hospital, and you don't want to go there ever again. I pop a couple pills and sit in Dad's chair to calm myself. We used to fight when I would get like this. Nothing physical, just a lot of shouting. I still feel guilty for putting them through all those years of pain and abuse. I didn't do it intentionally. I didn't ask to be this way. At least now I have an outlet. The hits are my therapy. I just need to be more careful from now on. I have to remain in control at all times.

I go for a walk with only my legal knife in my pocket. I put my hands in the pockets of my coat and hold the knife handle with my left hand. It's mid-April and I can hear the birds singing. It hasn't rained the last couple days which pleases me. The air is still chill on my shaved head. I pull my coat tight around my body like a bat folding its wings. I imagine myself as a mountain lion stalking its territory. My body has grown lean and more powerful. I've been watching the news to see if they've found the body of the fisherman. I've been inside mostly since that night and the river is several blocks behind my house. Maybe I'll ask Saint Nick tomorrow.

The next afternoon Saint Nick is at the door with my package. He's curious about it but I keep my lips tight. We chat about the weather. Getting nice outside, he says. Yeah, I've always liked this time of year. New life, new hope, I say. He smiles and waves goodbye. Til tomorrow! He says. I take the package inside and sit on the couch. I unbox the boots and try them on. It'll take a while to break them in but they fit nice. Quality leather with a nice shine to it, and the treads are a different pattern than my last pair. I'll start wearing these when I'm not out on the job. I'll stick with my Merrell's for the hits. I'll keep them hidden in the basement.

I forgot to ask Nick about the killing. He didn't mention any murder so they must not have found the body yet. They're in for a surprise. That man's head is porridge. I go online and chat with my virtual lady friends. I've always been a huge flirt. There's maybe ten girls that I talk with regularly. I like to pretend that I'm a sophisticated gentleman. They think I'm so sweet. I help them with their problems and listen to their troubles. I'm a good listener. I would have made a good priest.

I've been watching videos on YouTube about kukri fighting. I'm getting pretty handy with it. It's a lot more complicated than the whack of an axe. It's a very beautiful weapon, the curve of the blade, the horn handle with its brass accents. Mine came directly from Nepal. The soldiers use them there. I've been thinking about the cathedral down at the end of the street. There are several priests who spew their poison from the pulpit there. I could easily pick them off one by one. Maybe even carve bloody crosses into their foreheads just for fun. The press would eat that up. If I go to confession I could do some damage in the booth but it'd be risky. Maybe I'll go to mass on Sunday and scope the place out. I haven't been in over 20 years.

I hang around the house til noon lounging and thinking. I sit down at the computer and type out a haiku: Lone mountain lion/Standing on a seaside cliff/Screaming at the wind. I post it on my social media profile. It gets a couple likes from writer friends. An hour later there's a knock at the door. It's Saint Nick, holding a large box, smiling ear to ear. Good day to you, I say to him. And to you as well, my liege, he says. We chuckle. Big package today, Nick says. I've been waiting, I say. I won't ask any questions, says Nick. Probably better for the both of us, I say. We laugh again and he hands me the box. We say our goodbyes and I close and lock the front door. I take the box to the couch and open it with my Buck knife, slitting the packaging tape and unfolding the cardboard flaps. Inside the box there appears to be a large pile of moss and dead leaves. It's the Ghillie suit. I take it out of the box and try it on. It's a little long in the legs but it'll do. I look at myself in the mirror and say, Yep, Swamp Thing. I take the suit off and put it back in the box. I'll be needing it later tonight.

When evening comes I begin mentally preparing myself. No screw ups this time. I have the Ghillie suit. I am Swamp Thing. I will become one with the river and its banks. I will come alive only to attack. I can do this. I believe in myself.

8 PM. I stuff the suit into a briefcase and put on my Merrell's. I'll change into my costume once I hit the banks. I wear casual clothes and take dad's old fishing pole out of the garage as a prop. I place the kukri into the briefcase with the suit. I leave the house, locking the door behind me. After a ten minute walk I reach the banks of the river. I find a good spot. No one is around. I suit up and disappear into the bushes along the walking trail. I wait. I wait some more. Nothing. I hold the kukri in my right hand to feel its heft. A few minutes later two women come into view, walking the trail headed right for me. They look to be in their 40s or 50s and are both fit. I pause to admire their aesthetic beauty. As they come within striking

distance, the bushes come alive with a flashing blade. I strike the first one in the neck, nearly decapitating her. Her friend screams and is about to run but I'm quicker. I bury the kukri into her back and she drops. Both dead. No one hears their screams except me. I take off the suit, stuff it into the briefcase, clean the kukri in the river, place it in the case. When I'm done I pick up dad's fishing pole and head back to the house.

I wake late the next morning. I allowed myself to sleep in as a reward for a job well done last night. Two birds with one kukri. Surely this will make the papers.

1 PM. Just been lounging around waiting for Nick. I'm watching the episode of *Batman: The Animated Series* where The Riddler traps Batman in a virtual reality world. Such a great cartoon. I used to watch it every weekday after school. There's a knock at the door, must be Saint Nick. I get up and walk over and open the door to find a very distressed Saint Nicholas. Have you heard? he says. Heard what? I say. There's been another murder, three murders, all along the banks of the Rouge! So they found ol' Porridge Head too, I think. It's all over the news! Nick says. They're calling him The Rouge River Killer now! Nick says. I stop and think, that's

not such a bad name but it's too similar to The Green River Killer. They can do better than that. I calmly reassure Nick that everything is going to be okay, that he doesn't deliver mail to the river, so he's not in danger. But Nick is still visibly shaken. He leaves without saying goodbye.

I sit on the couch and feel sorry for Saint Nick. I didn't mean to scare him. The cows, yes, but not Nick. I have to stay focused. High profile project coming up and it starts on Sunday. I'm going to put on my Sunday best, trim my beard, shave my head, and join the herd for mass. I'll take a camera with me and say I'm a photographer shooting old churches. I don't think they'll mind. They might even grant me access to areas restricted to the public, which is what I'm after. I need to know the ins and outs of those pedophiles. Probably going to use a garrote and pick them off one by one. I think there's only three of them. If I space it out enough I should be able to score a hat trick. This is going to attract big attention, maybe even national press coverage, so I have to get it down to a science. I'll shoot the pictures on Sunday, might even get friendly with the priests. It'll only help me if they trust me.

Just going to take it easy for the next few days to prepare for Sunday. I hope I'm not a nervous wreck; I don't like being in crowds. They kept the churches open so the faithful could ask god to make the virus go away but they set a limit on attendance to prevent the spread. I'm sitting in Dad's chair looking out the window with a lozenge in my mouth. It's minty fresh, and bursting with sweet nicotine.

5 PM. The house is quiet like it always is, except for when I'm blaring music. I'm sitting reading a magazine trying to think of something productive to do. I could carve. I'm pretty burnt out on the knife after the lion head though and am sick of doing wood spirits, even though they remind me of Dad. I text Rose to see if she's available. No response. I go online and browse antique katana on eBay. I own one from WWII. My phone makes its text noise. I go over to it and it's Rose. She'd been busy cooking dinner, chicken n dumplings. Rose would make a great wife. When I tell her that she laughs. I tell her about the double murder and how the press has dubbed me The Rouge River Killer. She says that has a nice ring to it. I tell her I don't like it and she texts me a sad face. It's alright, after my next big project they'll come up with some other crazy name for me, I tell her. I don't go into any detail about my plans. I want it to be a surprise, for everyone, even Rose.

The next few days pass uneventfully. Today is Saturday. Tomorrow is the big photoshoot. I dig through the basement until I find my old Canon Rebel that I bought used on eBay several years ago. I charge it up and reacquaint myself with the different functions. I should be good. I pick out a nice, unassuming outfit to wear, and find Dad's old trenchcoat. I try it on. It's a little big in the shoulders but it will have to do. It's camel hair which is a nice, neutral color and I want to look as unintimidating as possible. I've let my hair grow out a little bit to appear less threatening. I'm good to go tomorrow morning.

Sunday. 10 AM. Mass begins in an hour. I've showered and trimmed my beard. Put on my photographer costume and am now sitting on the couch, waiting. I keep reminding myself that I'm only going to take pictures. I'll have to socialize a bit but I can be fake when it's needed. The walk to the cathedral is pleasant; there are others walking toward it across the street. I'm trying to maintain a cheerful, positive attitude. I wave to the cows and they wave back. I'm a good, friendly neighbor. I reach the cathedral and walk inside. A priest stands in the vestibule to greet us. I ask him if I would be allowed to take some pictures of the beautiful windows and architecture and he smiles and tells me to enjoy myself, and that I am welcome here.

I take out the Canon and begin shooting. Stained glass, paintings, statues, candles, everything. The altar is about 200 feet tall, I remember Dad telling me. I take a picture. Mass begins and I sit down in a pew, genuflecting first. I pop a lozenge and listen to the rant in disgust. The priest conducting Mass is fat and piggish and his skin is a lovely shade of pink. I take a picture. I recognize the welcoming priest off to the side. An older priest with a long beard and glasses stands beside him. I take a picture. After about an hour Mass ends and the herd begins to move out. I approach the welcoming priest and ask him if he'd be willing to give me a tour of the cathedral. Happily, he says.

He shows me the windows and the tile floor, adding his own commentary along the way. I take more pictures. He tells me about the altar, that it is actually on wheels. That surprises me. I ask him if we can go behind the altar. He is reluctant at first but eventually he agrees. He leads me into a sort of Mass preparation room, with cassocks hanging on racks, unconsecrated hosts in packages, chalices, other items needed for the big celebration. I pay close attention to the exits but I don't take any more pictures. I don't want to arouse suspicion.

We finish the tour and I thank the priest graciously. He smiles and tells me to come back any Sunday. I will, I say. Perhaps I will. I check the camera. Sixty-five photos taken. Sixty-five photos that will soon be deleted. I only came to see the back room. That's where the priests get ready for services. That's where they're vulnerable. They're all old and weak; I could probably take out all three in five minutes. I can't be arrogant though. This will be my biggest hit. I have to plan it out to the last detail. Luckily, I have all the time in the world.

I walk home with the herd and chat a little bit with an old woman. She's conservative but friendly. She tells me about everything the president is doing to stop the spread of the virus. I just smile and nod. A hammer would look good in her brains. I reach my house and wave goodbye to the moo cows. The house is quiet and dark how I like it. I can think in peace. I have a lot of thinking to do over the next few weeks, maybe longer. I need to talk to Rose. She'll help me figure out a way to get this job done.

5 PM. Spent the last few hours on the couch wracking my brain. I go online and find Rose. I tell her that I need help and tell her my ideas. She thinks I'm being unrealistic and that I would need to do it with a gun. I ask her about doing it with

two kukris, and tell her that it would all take place within a confined space, that people would hear gunshots. She stops to consider this and says that it might work if I can do it fast and get out of there. When I tell her about the exits in the back of the cathedral she gets excited. Do it, she says. I'll have to order another kukri, I say, but that's no big deal. I'm going to wait a while and do some smaller hits as Swamp Thing before making the big kill in the church.

I order another kukri from the same maker as my old one and am searching for some kind of leather holster so I don't carry them into the church with my hands like an amateur. I end up finding leather holsters that attach to the sides of a belt which is perfect if I wear Dad's camel hair trench coat. I order a surgical mask just to be safe. In Viral World everyone wears masks; it's a murderer's paradise. It's getting late. I decide to watch a movie. I find *The Adventures of Baron Munchausen* on Netflix, sit back, and relax. I've seen it a dozen times, but it's still a favorite. Same director as Brazil, my all-time favorite. Terry Gilliam from Monty Python is a genius. I half pay attention to the film but my mind is racing with thoughts of violence. The swing of the hatchet, the splatter, the bodies hitting the ground. I'll think more on it tomorrow morning.

7 AM Steak and eggs. Do a little light cleaning, sharpen my dad's carving knives on the leather, just keeping myself busy. I'm setting small tasks for myself in an attempt to maintain some degree of focus. I'm feeling manicky even though I ate a psychotropic salad. I try to sit down but can't. Have to keep moving. Have to keep swimming like a shark or I'll go belly up. Maybe I'll do a hit tonight. It's been a while since the Rouge River Killer struck. Gotta give the local newsmedia something to talk about. Saint Nick knocks at the door with my package, the second kukri. I paid extra for overnight shipping. He's still terrified. First the virus, now the killer, he says. Tough times, I say, keep your head up. I tell him to live long and prosper while making the Vulcan salute and he laughs nervously, then leaves.

I sit down, my leg shaking uncontrollably, and open the box. It's the exact same kukri as my other one so I'm not too excited. I am excited about attempting to dual wield them, like in a video game. I wonder if this is going to work or if I'm being fantastical. Rose was optimistic about it. I go online and watch kukri fighting videos and practice with my two blades. I'm starting to feel pumped again. The hypomania is giving me confidence and a sense of raw power. I'll have to keep practicing, like I did with my throwing axes. Maybe I'll dig those out and go down to the river tonight, suit up in the Ghillie, lace up my killing boots. It's good that I've given the cows some time to settle back into their quiet lives of complacency. It's time to startle the herd again.

At around 11 PM I took down another fisherman on the riverbank. Nothing spectacular to report about it. It was an easy kill. I was Swamp Thing in the bushes behind him, threw an axe which lodged itself in his back, then slit his throat. Not very satisfying but it was a very successful hit. I'm becoming bored with the river killings though. What thrills me now is the prospect of the cathedral triple murder. I've leveled up and am ready for it, just need more practice with the kukris until I'm proficient. It'll take a few weeks to hone my skills. I'm looking meaner and leaner and fighting machiner these days. I hated being out of shape. Killing is proving to be cost-effective. Cheaper than buying a gym membership.

1 AM. I'm not going to sleep tonight. The thoughts are still racing and the fantasies more violent. Fields of babies screaming and being tortured. Bodies hanging from hooks. I'm imagining my face on the cover of books. I wonder who will play me in the movie. For any of this to happen though, I

would have to eventually get caught. Maybe being caught wouldn't be so bad. This house is already a prison.

I feel strange. Sometimes I feel disconnected from my body, like a floating brain. It's hard to control my movements at times. Side effects of the medication. I walk funny now too; my left leg makes a semicircular motion when I take a step with it. I'm often tripping over myself. I have to be very aware of my body when I'm working. When I'm sitting my right leg shakes up and down. I have facial ticks. I'll squeeze my eyes shut hard or scrunch up my face. It's all side effects of the medication. I've complained to the doctor about it but he says I either take the pills or I'll end up in the hospital again. I don't want that.

I still haven't slept. Haven't eaten either. I'm not hungry. Been doing pushups and situps to pass the time. I don't want to tell the doctor that I'm manic because I've been so productive lately. I want it to continue. I think about the big hit coming up. Maybe if I bought a black cassock and wore it they'd think I was a new priest. I don't think the priest who gave me the tour would recognize me if I'm wearing my surgical mask. I'll have to cut my beard short in order to wear it. I could say I was sent by another parish to see the beautiful cathedral. I sit down, find a Catholic retail supply site, and order the cassock.

Saint Nick shows up at 2; he's in better spirits. Trying to keep a positive attitude in these shit times, he says with a sarcastic grin. I smile and take today's mail. There's a notice from Social Security reminding me to fill out and send back my paperwork or I will stop receiving payments. I get worried and sit down at the kitchen table with the forms, quickly filling them out. I have to describe my daily life, which makes me chuckle, along with providing a list of medications, doctors' names, contact information. I complete the forms and stick them in the envelope provided. Glad that's done. Just have to walk to the mailbox and dump the envelope inside and I'll be all set for the next few months.

The temperature is rising. It's late April. The house is dark but tidy. I don't like leaving the lights on during the day, even if it's raining. I save money that way and it's just my personal preference. I like the dark. I've always been a night owl, and when I'm in a psychosis, I'm a day and night owl. Once went one full week without any sleep, back when I was a teenager. My psychiatric problems are nothing new; it all started in high school when I was first diagnosed. I never told any doctor about my true thoughts though. I've heard you get locked up if you do that.

I'm calmer now. Probably because I'm sleep-deprived. I feel dizzy and disconnected from my body again. No kukri practice today. No reading either. I'll probably just lie on the couch and watch movies until I hopefully pass out. I sit on the couch and think about all the murders, the virus, the "Rouge River Killer." I wonder how Saint Nick is really doing, and Rose too. I'll try to find her online later today. I need to know she's okay.

8 PM. I was able to nap for a couple of hours. I didn't end up watching any movies. There's nothing I feel like watching right now. I'm online window shopping normie clothing and talking to Rose. I ask her for help deciding on what clothes to buy. She has the same fashion sense as I do, which is basically Serial Killer Chic, so we're both struggling to find upright citizen clothes for men. I'm looking at linen slacks, Hawaiian shirts, sandals. When I ask her how she's doing she says okay, that times are tough all around, she says, but that she and her boyfriend are surviving. She asks me what trouble I've gotten myself into now and I say no comment with a smiley face. I'm

not taking any chances, even with Rose. The Cathedral Killing must remain a secret until it comes to pass.

I'm watching *Ghost Dog: Way of the Samurai* with Forest Whitaker, directed by Jim Jarmusch. Another favorite. Right now Ghost Dog is on the rooftop practicing with his katana which reminds me that I have to start practicing with the kukris again tomorrow. My mind starts to drift again. Mom and Dad used to watch movies on this TV. Mom would sit next to me on the couch, and dad in his chair next to the window. That part of my life is over, though, and I've got to keep moving. I can't afford to be sentimental right now.

I slept through the night, and am blasting Tori Amos' *Little Earthquakes* album. Bowie's *Scary Monsters* is next on the playlist. I think I'll watch *Labyrinth* today for the 3,000th time. At one point in my life I wanted to work in the Creature Shop in London, but that was an unrealistic dream. A dream of a boy raised on *Sesame Street*. *Scary Monsters* starts up. I practice my kukri slashes while "Ashes to Ashes" plays all around me. I sing along in my raspy voice.

Saint Nick is at the door with more junk mail; a fly fishing catalogue for Dad. Saint Nick is doing well. There haven't been any killings recently so he's feeling more confident about his safety and that of his family. We chat a little and he gives me updates on the global spread of the virus. Nick calls the president an Ass Muppet which makes me laugh. I'm not all that political but I do hate the president.

I throw the mail into the wastebasket and go online. I chat and flirt with my virtual girlfriends, reassuring them that everything is going to be okay. You can't live your life in a state of panic, I tell them. You have to remain calm and focused. These are the words I tell myself. I'm not in an online relationship with any of these women; I tried that a few times and it always failed. But we chat and call each other cute names and exchange pictures, so there is something romantic about it. Rose is different. She's my Hellwife and someday we will meet in person and it will be glorious.

The next day Saint Nick comes bearing gifts. He tells me that there have been four more killings in the neighborhood but the police are still baffled. He says that they believe all the killings are the work of one person, whom the press have now officially dubbed The Rouge River Killer. My skin prickles and I try to stifle a smile. Nick is scared but he tries not to show it. He hands me a package which I take to the couch. I slit the box open with my Buck knife and unfold the flaps. It's my cassock. It's a perfect fit. I look handsome in it. I take it off and hang it in the vestibule closet, along with our jackets. I kept all of Mom and Dad's clothes. I couldn't bear the thought of some stranger wearing them if I donated them to the Salvation Army.

I practice with the kukris while blasting Nirvana's demo tape. I've idolized Kurt Cobain since high school. He would have made a good killer I think. It's too bad he didn't take out his wife.

I'm becoming skilled with the two kukris. I'm confident in my ability and believe the big hit will be a success. My only concern is the aftermath. There will be a huge investigation, and the neighborhood is already in full circus mode from the four recent killings. I've been watching the flashing red and blue lights out the front window. Saint Nick says it's all over the news. I've lost count of the bodies. I'm not a numbers guy, but I know my achievements are stacking up. I'm not stopping anytime soon.

When I stopped by the grocery store the place was packed. I almost had a panic attack from the crowds. All the toilet paper and paper towels were gone. No hand sanitizer either. The cows are doomsday prepping. I know I will survive. And if I don't, I won't care. Neither will anyone else. Poor Rose will never even know if I'm gone. I better message her today. I've been growing more concerned about the virus. Saint Nick told me that it mutated into a more deadly strain. I've been ignoring the media and not buying into the hysteria until now. I better stay in the house for a while. Maybe I should postpone the big hit.   The churches are probably closed anyway. Everything is these days.

It's 6 PM and I'm watching the national news on channel 4. The virus is a much bigger deal than I thought. Borders are closed, the global economy is crumbling, some people are taking to the streets. Soon it will be anarchy unless a vaccine is discovered. I've always said that the herd could use a culling; Rose says that too. Mass panic is underway, and the cows are self-isolating. This makes me laugh because I've self-isolated my whole life. They're complaining on social media about toilet paper shortages and the dreaded silence of their homes. What a bunch of babies. Let the virus come; it will only aid me in my task. If the herd is panicked it's less likely that a few bodies in the river will be noticed.

The elderly are dying off in the neighborhood. That church going conservative old cow of a woman is dead. Nick told me all this when he delivered the mail yesterday. A lot of kids are sick and stuck at home. People aren't walking their dogs anymore. No one's fishing the river after the killings were reported. I don't know what to do with myself. The thoughts and urges are still there but now I have no outlet. Maybe I'll carve a gnome for Dad. He always loved gnomes. He kind of looked like one himself.

I'm watching documentaries about serial killers. They're fairly uninteresting people; I don't identify with most of them; my parents loved me and I was never abused. I still like Ed Gein because of his craftsmanship. Maybe I should start taking trophies from my kills. I think that's too gruesome even for me. Down the basement, I take a block of bass wood and start roughing out a form with Dad's knives. The body first, then the head and the tall, pointy hat. I chip away at the block for a few hours until the form of the gnome is recognizable. I begin the detail work on the face and torso. I give the gnome a hatchet in his belt as an inside joke. I work late into the night until the gnome is finished and set it on dad's work desk. Just a little gift from a loving son.

I decide I need to sleep. I plug my phone into the charger. I take out my contact lenses. I eat my psychotropic salad. The nightly ritual of your friendly neighborhood serial killer. I think I'll be able to sleep tonight. I lay down in my bed, the sheets stained with sweat. I'll have to wash them soon. My thoughts keep me awake for another hour until I finally pass out. I dream of dead cows.

I rise at 4 AM. I should be getting my next paycheck soon. I'm running low on funds. The house is paid off, I don't own a vehicle, I don't have many expenses other than food, pills, and work tools. I go online. Rose isn't up at this hour, plus she's in another time zone. I look at Damascus steel kukris on eBay and then open the church's website. There's a ton of information, including a photo map of the grounds. Idiots. This is too easy. The rectory is located behind the cathedral. That's where the priests live and sleep. I've never broken into a building but it's all laid out on the map, the entrances and exits. It should be no trouble. Maybe I'll take a crucifix as a souvenir.

All my practicing was for naught. I don't need the kukris for this job. I can just use a knife and cut their throats while they sleep. I'd prefer to butcher them like pigs but that would be too risky. Maybe I'll take one kukri, 3 slashes, 3 kills. I know how to pick a lock so that won't be a problem. Dad taught me. Still, the fantasy of the dual wielding kukri killer lingers. I'll save that for another job.   Perhaps when I go after the Trumpers. The rat bastard won a second term and everybody's suffering the effects of his incompetence in handling the virus crisis. Mom and Dad are dead because of his orange monkey ass.

2:36 PM. Saint Nick knocks at the front door. He delivers the junk and we chat for a bit, mostly about the progress of the virus and our dipshit president. It's good to talk to a fellow liberal again. Mom and Dad were staunch Democrats and they influenced my own politics. Rose is socially liberal but she doesn't trust big government and is a gun nut. I tease her about that all the time. She's more of an anarcho-survivalist. I get that. During past psychoses I've doomsday prepped the house and garage, so she and I will both be fine. I pity the fool who tries to break into my house. They'll quickly receive a sharp blow to the head and a swim in the river.

Rose and her boyfriend are having money problems. With her not working, their income was cut in half, and she's still struggling to find a way to make money. She started selling her paintings on Etsy but she's having trouble drawing attention to her work. She's resourceful though and will find a way. You're a survivor and you'll manage, I tell her. She asks about me and how I've been doing and I tell her that I'm in a mild manic episode and then I tell her about the dog walkers I took out. She praises my courage and determination. Kill all the fuckers, she says. After serving unruly customers for years, Rose has become a genuine misanthrope. She hasn't killed anybody, but she easily could if she wanted.

8:45 PM. Cook eggs, eat, swallow pills, shit. Sharpen the kukris. I decided to take both since I've been practicing so hard. I couldn't wait any longer so I've decided to make the strike tonight. I leave at midnight. Have a few hours to kill. I lay on the couch and remember Catholic school. The verbal and physical abuse from the teachers, the bullying from classmates, the priests with their cold, withered hands. They never molested me but there were others they did. The sickness and depravity of it. It makes my stomach turn.

Time to get ready. I put on my pea coat and camouflage balaclava. Everyone is wearing a mask these days so I won't look unusual to anyone should I be seen. I strap the kukris to my chest with the leather harness I ordered last week and button up the coat. I find Dad's old lock picking kit in the basement and stuff it in my pocket. I lace up my killing boots, which I clean thoroughly after every hit. I'm ready. I open the door, locking it behind me, and make my way out into the night.

No one is on the streets. I look like a cliché killer but so does everyone in Viral World. I casually walk toward the cathedral, looking at the pristine suburban homes and the brand new Ford vehicles in the driveways. Most of the men in the neighborhood are Ford workers, engineers mostly. I'll pick them off one by one in due time. My heart is pounding. I'm trying to remain calm. I slow my breathing to decrease my heart rate. I'm meditating. When I reach the cathedral I walk around to the back to where the rectory is located. None of the lights are on, inside or out, which is good. I take out the kit from my pocket and pick the lock on the front door. Darkness inside. It smells like a funeral home. All I can hear is the ticking of the large grandfather clock in the corner. I move quietly throughout the house, going up the stairs to reach the three bedrooms. So far, so good. The bedroom doors are not locked so I enter the first one. Under the covers of the bed is the fat, piggish priest who said Mass. I stop to stare at him in disgust. I remove one kukri from my chest harness, grasp it in my fist, lift it over my head, and make a swift, decisive stroke into the head of the priest. I make his head into a vagina. It is rather messy but I won't be here when they come to clean him up. I repeat this process for the next two rooms, first the welcoming priest with a slash to the throat, and finally Methuselah, half asleep and mumbling prayers as I open his belly. Three slashes, three kills, just as I had planned. I make my way back down the stairs and exit the rectory wondering how long it will be before the bodies are discovered.

The whole process took no more than 15 minutes, including the time it took me to walk to and from the rectory. It's now after midnight. I'm high on adrenaline. I put Robyn in the CD player and blast *Body Talk*, singing and moving to the beat. I switch the TV on to a nature documentary about grizzly bears. I need stimulation right now. I won't be sleeping tonight. I'm going to be famous. I can't wait to see Saint Nick; he'll have news. Maybe not tomorrow but surely the day after. I hop online and find Rose and tell her what I just did. She's shocked with joy. She hates organized religion and pedophile priests. She's so happy for me. We chat for an hour, then she goes to bed. I watch a grizzly bear tear the head off a fish on TV.

2:47 AM. I'm still bouncing off the walls. I had originally planned to go after the right wingers next but that might be too large scale a project, one that would surely attract national attention. I'm not ready for that yet. I have to figure out a way to get downtown. I'm going to wreak havoc on the art school down there, the one that ruined me as an artist. Wait, the school is closed due to the virus. Damn, I say to myself. Still, I'm sure I could locate the two professors who conducted my portfolio review. They're the ones who ruined me. They must be old now. Or retired. Or maybe even dead. One was already old when I was a student there 20 years ago. I hope he's not dead; I want his death to be a pleasure all my own.

6 AM. Still high on bloodlust. I ate a couple bananas and a protein bar for breakfast. Then I did some pushups. They're difficult for me to do due to an old work injury in my shoulders, but I manage. I eat the pill salad despite not wanting to. I don't want anything bringing me down from this. Don't know if it's the mania or the killings, but I'm flying high. The Rouge River Killer is about to get a lot of press coverage. Saint Nick should be by around 1 or 2, so I have hours to kill. I turn on the local news and it's all Viral World hysteria; no mention of any killings which disappoints me. I sit on the couch with my Plumb, snapping it back and forth with my

wrist, testing the edge of the blade against my fingertips. It could use a sharpening. I take out the file and leather and get to work until the blade can slice easily through my doctor's business card. I owe him a phone call. I've been so busy that I forgot all about him, but I'll need refills soon. I'll do that later.

It's noon. Nick should be here soon. I haven't watched the morning news. I've been practicing with the kukris and watching demonstrations on YouTube. I'm brimming with physical energy so I've been playing my music loud and cleaning the house. I can't contain my excitement. I killed three filthy Jesuits. This will definitely send a message to the Church; I hope it reaches the Vatican. The Pope would be the ultimate target along with Trump, but that's fantastical thinking. They're way too well-protected. I'm just one man. But I am the terror of this suburb. I'm the fucking Rouge River Killer and I won't stop til there's a bullet in my head.

A knock at the door. Saint Nick has a look of horror on his face. Have you seen the morning news? he asks. I've been cleaning up the house, I tell him. He goes on to tell me that the bodies of three parish priests were found slaughtered in their beds. They were found by the cleaning lady who came to the rectory early this morning, he tells me. Catholics all over the country are up in arms, many claiming that it was the work of a Muslim terrorist, since there is a large Muslim population on the east side of town. I fake shock and concern. Nick isn't religious but his wife is a Catholic, and she goes to the cathedral every Sunday for Mass. She knew those priests, he tells me. They were her confessors and they baptized Nick's children. Suddenly a feeling of remorse comes prickling over my skin but I ignore it. I tell Nick that it was probably just some psychopath that had been molested by a priest. Nick says he thinks it's the Rouge River Killer. I say that anything is possible and take the mail and throw it in the garbage.

I shouldn't feel bad for Nick and his wife. It's unprofessional. There must still be some humanity left in me. I'll have to choke it out until it's dead. That's the only way I'll be able to continue. I look over to the mantle at the mountain lion head. The mountain lion doesn't pity the deer it kills; it kills to eat. I kill to calm the thoughts in my head. I don't know where they come from; they've always just been there. The doctor would say it's the illness, but why do I enjoy killing? It's something to think about further, but not right now. I seek peace, and someday, I'll retire if I'm not caught first. But that day is not today. I have much more work to do.

3 PM. I need some air. I get up off the couch and walk outside and sit in the chair by the garage. I look at the tall oaks, the flowers that are beginning to blossom. I listen to the birds singing and the woodpeckers pecking, while black and gray squirrels chase each other up the trees. All this wretched beauty before me when all I see is eventual ruin. I miss winter when the world is black and white and people slip and fall on the ice and break bones. I like cold weather; the cold that buries itself deep beneath your flesh to the core of your bones. Children should be playing in the streets but instead they're locked inside their homes. The cows should be at restaurants feeding and getting drunk at bars. All closed down. The herd is finding isolation troubling, according to what I read on the internet. Welcome to my world, I say to them.

Maybe I'll have a fire tonight, I tell myself. Dad's rusty old firepit sits in the middle of the yard, unused since he died. There's some firewood piled up along the side of the garage. I think I'll spend the rest of the day outside for a change of pace. I pop a lozenge and walk inside the house for a moment to grab an NA beer, then take it back out to my chair. I'm wearing jeans and a flannel so I'm warm enough. I left my pea coat and hat inside the house. I enjoy nature, the little bit of it I have in the backyard. I always wanted to build a shack up in the U.P. and be a hermit woodsman. I still fantasize about that sometimes. Living off the grid, deep in the north woods, no one around to bother me. All alone in the deep, dark woods. The thought of this pleases me.

I've been out here for four hours and it's getting a little cold. I think I'll start the fire up. I go inside the house and take junk mail out of the garbage, grab the rest of the NA's, and head back outside. I dump all the catalogues into the pit and light it with my Zippo, a souvenir I kept from my smoking days. I pile brush on top, then wood, and fan the flames with an *Orvid* catalogue. Soon the pit is roaring with orange, dancing light. I move the garage chair close to the firepit and drink another NA. NA Labatt is my favorite, good enough to keep me from drinking the real stuff, so I always pick up a 12 pack when I go to the store. I don't think anyone else buys it, which is fine with me. Let the cows destroy their livers with alcohol. It just makes them easier targets.

I put the fire out at midnight and go back inside, carrying the empty cans with me. It was good to be outside; I feel rejuvenated from the clean air. Inside it's dark so I light a few candles in the living room. I go online and chat with Rose. I don't know what to do next, I tell her. Keep going, she says, you're on a roll! I tell her about the two art professors I want to take out and she tells me to lay low until the cathedral killing hysteria dies down. Apparently the news has reached Iowa. Everyone is on lockdown now due to the spread of the virus, and it's rumored that the president will soon declare martial law. If that happens I won't be able to leave the house at all. Rose is concerned but unafraid. I'm a little nervous. I get my news from Saint Nick and he's been panic-stricken the last few days. I'm going to have to find some less violent hobbies.

I can't sleep so I do some shopping. I decided that I'd like to take up archery as a hobby, so I log onto eBay to look at bows. I order a used Samick Sage recurve bow from a reputable seller, along with practice arrows. I also win an auction for a Damascus steel kukri, a gift to myself for the successful cathedral killing. Only had to spend 30 dollars on it. I hope no one is monitoring my online shopping habits. That could be very bad for me. But at least now I have packages to look forward to receiving, and Saint Nick will be excited for me like he always is. I hope his family is doing alright.

The bow, arrows, and kukri will arrive in a week, so I'll have to keep myself occupied somehow until then. So many people are dying from the virus that the Rouge River Killer has mostly been forgotten. I'm itching to get back out there. I've been watching a little bit of Local 4 news and the dumb cows are hoarding supplies again, especially paper products. Who would have guessed that in the midst of global catastrophe, toilet paper would become the most sought after commodity. The gun nuts are stockpiling shotguns and ammo because this, they believe, is the work of the government after all. For a moment I feel sad but the sadness quickly turns to disgust. I hope Rose isn't losing her mind. I'll check in on her tomorrow.

3 AM. I'm watching *12 Monkeys* and eating hunter sausage. Carving another wood spirit for Dad and making a mess of wood chips on the coffee table which I'll clean up later. Just trying to stay stimulated. Morphine plays on the stereo. I'm reminded of my old life before the killings, when I would stay in the house all day by myself doing nothing. Laying on the couch and staring at the walls, studying the pictures of buildings my dad hung on them. I burned the big sunflower oil pastel that Mom loved so much because I always hated it. Now I'm looking at the mountain lion carving and feeling the urge. I wish I was an animal so I didn't have to feel these human feelings.

I go to bed at 5 AM and sleep for four hours, a deep, dreamless sleep. When I wake up I brush my teeth and take a shower. It's been a few days and I'm getting ripe. The ice cold spray shocks my mind and body as I lather and rinse. After I shower, I eat a simple breakfast of eggs and orange juice, then go online to read about the panic. The cows are posting virus memes to distract themselves from the seriousness of the outbreak. They can't build coffins fast enough to keep up with demand. I think about Saint Nick and his family. I wish I could give him a hug. He's been wearing a mask on his route along with gloves. I miss seeing his smile. He tries to put up a chipper front but the virus has changed him. It's changed the world.

The rest of the week passes slowly as I wait for my packages. I've been researching recurve bow target shooting and watching demonstration videos on YouTube. It keeps me busy. At 1:46 PM there's a knock at the front door. Good Saint Nicholas, come bearing gifts. Three large packages. I know he's smiling behind the mask because I can see the wrinkles form around his eyes. Heard the new Radiohead record? he asks. No, haven't gotten around to it yet, I say. It's great, Nick says, reminds me of *OK Computer*. I tell him I'll check it out when I get a chance. I tell him to stay safe and take care of his family. He thanks me and walks on.

I tear open the packages with my kukri. The first box is the arrows, cheap black plastic shafts with blunt points. They'll do fine for practice. Next I open the Damascus steel kukri. It's a work of art. Two tone horn handle with a beautiful rippling steel blade that looks like ocean waves. I grasp it in my fist and snap my wrist back and forth. It has a good feel to it. I'll be using it in the future. Then I open the largest box, slitting the tape with my Buck knife and unfolding the tall cardboard flaps. It's the Samick Sage. Elegantly crafted wood that fits nicely in the palm of my hand. I stand up with the bow and fix the bowstring so it's taut, then I fire an arrow across the room and into the wall. It bounces off and leaves a mark in the paint. This is going to be fun, I think to myself. I'll set up another piece of plywood out back and use it as a target. I destroyed the other plywood sheet with my axes.

I go outside and pull out the plywood from the garage. I lean it against the bushes lining the fence, then I walk back to the back door of the house with the bow and an arrow, draw the string, take aim, and fire. The arrow lodges itself in the plywood. Didn't hit the target I spraypainted on it but at least

I hit the wood. I try again. I continue practicing throughout the rest of the day, stopping only for a quick snack and a lozenge. I imagine myself as Robin Hood, molesting the fat, rich pigs, feeding the poor and downtrodden. I do have a special place in my heart for those in need, especially the disabled and minority groups. I hate all the rest, especially the dumb cows in this suburban wasteland. Once this virus passes the doors of the slaughterhouse will be flung back wide open.

The bow and arrow isn't new to me. I used to shoot when I was in Boy Scouts, but that was many years ago. I was good at it back then, and even though I'm rusty now I know I'll get better. I'll be firing arrows like Legolas soon enough. When I become an expert marksman maybe I'll even use the bow in my work. There are deer in the woods around the Rouge River. I could practice shooting a moving target. The mountain lion preys on deer.

7 AM the next morning. I have 12 arrows and half of them are busted to bits. I'll have to order more. Been shooting for two hours. I go inside to take a break and eat psychotropic salad. I only eat when I'm hungry. Dad used to cook huge meals for dinner and we would always end up wasting half of it. Mom cooked just for the three of us. I never cooked until I started

living alone. I use a large cast iron skillet for everything. It's heavy and black and would make a great weapon.

I watch bow hunting videos online. I'm going to have to hit that target a hundred more times before I attempt to take down a deer. Hunting animals is more difficult than I thought, especially with a recurve. When Rose signs on, she messages me to say that she's dying of boredom. Iowa is on lockdown. I tell her to paint something, the Gurkha man from her dreams maybe. She thanks me for the idea and says she'll get right on it after we're done talking. I tell her that I've been bored lately too, though I've taken up archery, and I got a new fancy Damascus steel kukri in the mail. She's excited and asks for pictures, so I take a few with my phone camera and send them to her. She's ecstatic. Happy Rose makes me happy, so I always aim to please her. Someday years from now we'll both be in hell as demon and whore.

I draw the bowstring until all my arrows are ruined, then go back inside and order five more packages of 12. I pay extra for rush delivery so I should have them by the day after next. What to do in the meantime. My disability payment was deposited into my account so apparently I filled out the forms correctly, assuring the government that I am indeed psychotic and unable to work. I haven't had a major depressive episode in years, so I think I'm over that part. Now it's just the anxiety and psychosis. That's what I'm being treated for by the doctor. I still haven't called him but his office would be closed anyway. Everything is closed now. I don't know what the cows are doing at home except posting memes on social media. The dog walkers are back out and I've been planning to break in my new Damascus. It hasn't drank yet. Soon it will be gulping down wine, dark and red.

The derelict students would be walking home from school now if school was in session. No mail today. I don't know if the post office is still delivering. I have no idea how bad things have gotten. I'll watch the news at 6. I hope I get my arrows. I enjoy shooting them. And I need to be practicing. Luckily the deer aren't on lockdown. I should go for a walk this evening after the news.

6 PM and I'm sitting on the couch with Local 4 on, lozenge tucked firmly in my cheek. The president is speaking, attempting to placate the herd, but I don't think anyone is buying it. Last week he was throwing toilet paper rolls into a crowd in Florida. Saint Nick was right about him being an Ass Muppet. Reporters are telling the cows to stay in their homes,

wash their hands constantly, and avoid any physical contact. The situation is worse than I thought. There is no mention of the Rouge River Killer and I'm a bit disappointed

Later that night, I'm ready for my walk. The only people on the streets are the dog walkers; I've been watching them out the front window. Easy prey, I think, and attach the sheath of my kukri to my belt, oil the blade, then slide it into the sheath. I put on my black pea coat and hat.

I think it's mid-April. The wind blows chill and the air is crisp. I walk down the steps of my front porch and into the streetlit darkness. The trees are black with no leaves yet, the streets slick with rain from a light afternoon shower. I plan to make only one hit tonight. I don't want to overdo it. I walk for several blocks at a leisurely pace, looking into the lit windows of the houses where the cows eat their cud. I can see them moving behind the windows, living their ordinary lives of loud desperation. When a runner comes into view I crouch down behind a parked car. She continues to approach until the flash of my kukri sends her head to the rainslick pavement. It hits the street like a ripe melon and rolls over on its side. The dumb cows leave their car doors unlocked in this neighborhood so I open a trunk and stuff her body and head into it, closing it gently so as not to draw attention.

The Damascus went through her neck like cream cheese. I'll have to order another one so I have two. Kinda wish I had kept the runner's head but I don't take trophies like Ed Gein. If the cops ever enter my home I don't want them finding body parts lying around. Or lampshades made from human skin. Or armchairs made out of human arms. It's not my aesthetic, or calling card. I like cozy and comfortable.

7 AM. Slept peacefully, no bad dreams. Eager to start practice this afternoon if the mail comes. I shave my head, brush my teeth, and weigh myself on the scale. 168 lbs. I've lost ten pounds. It feels good to be getting back in shape. My clothes fit better now too. I'm glad I stopped drinking beer and lost that obscene gut. I was self-conscious of my appearance for years. I think now some might even call me handsome. That makes me happy.

I go online at 8:40 hoping to find Rose. She's online so I message her that I've lost ten pounds and she begs for a picture, so I take one in the mirror and send it to her. She says

I'm hot and I laugh.   I'm glad she finds me attractive.
Someday in hell, I tell myself. We'll burn together, forever.

At 10 AM the rains begin, washing away all traces of the
previous night's crime. For once I'm happy to see it rain. I sit
in Dad's chair and look out the front window with a lozenge in
my mouth and a ginger beer in hand. Even if the arrows come,
there will be no practice today.

No mail. No Saint Nick. No arrows. I'm beginning to think
that buying a bow was a bad idea. If I can't get arrows, it's
useless. I'll just have to see how things progress and hopefully
the post office will reopen soon. I'll check the news tonight. I
miss my packages. I miss Saint Nick.

I spend the rest of the day inside as rain pours down. I drink
NA beer and eat hunter sausages for lunch and listen to The
Violent Femmes. I miss 90's music. I remember listening to
the FM radio stations in high school, as I'd sit at my drafting
table and draw dragons and monsters. Mom and Dad would
be downstairs reading or watching TV. I wish I didn't have
these memories; I wish they could be erased. I don't want to
remember. I have to keep moving forward or else I'll get
bogged down in the past and spiral into darkness.

Being on lockdown isn't helping. Now that the post office has closed, I can't order anything online. I'm going to run out of damned toilet paper. I need my work tools. I need my damned arrows. And I need to see Saint Nick and make sure he and his family are safe. Hundreds of people are dying every day in this country and I'm completely cut off from everyone, except for Rose. She's the one person I still have. I wonder if she decided to paint again. She has told me several times about the man in her dreams, the Gurkha man who teaches her things. She's painted his portrait twice now. I want to see the third portrait.

I put on a movie and try to relax. *Pee Wee's Big Adventure*, that'll cheer me up. I'm a loner and a rebel too, Dottie. I eat a protein bar and watch for a half hour, then lose focus and begin sharpening the Plumb. Haven't used it in while, but after taking that cow's head off with the Damascus, I'm starting to prefer kukris over axes. I never thought I'd say that. I was the Hatchet Man once. The Rouge River Killer uses a variety of tools, and is a master of disguise and improvisation. I'm a mystical ninja.

6 PM. I turn on the news and stare at the panic. No mention of the post offices being closed though, so maybe I just haven't

had any mail the last couple days. It's happened before. The rain is still raining with no sign of letting up, so it's going to be another quiet evening at home. I go downstairs to the carving station. I take a big block off the shelf and start carving not knowing what I'm making. I work for a couple hours until I have an abstract sculpture in my hands that resembles my own face and head, with deep rivers streaking across the flesh.

From 9 to 11 PM I practice with the kukris, leaving the Plumb and the Damascus to talk amongst themselves. I used to train in the martial arts, ninjutsu and jujutsu, but never weapons training. I don't need a class for that; YouTube is my master. At midnight I lay down on the couch and pop a lozenge. I'm excited about the future. I wish I knew how many kills I've made. When they find the body in the trunk, the Killer will be back on the news. I'll have to keep an eye out.

2 PM the next day. A knock at the door. It's Saint Nick. We're both happy to see each other, and he has a large package for me. Turns out he wasn't feeling well the last few days and the post office couldn't find anyone to cover his route. He was worried it was the virus but he's feeling better now. I tell him not to die on me because I need him for my deliveries. Is that all I'm good for? he jokes. We laugh and chat a bit about the

cathedral killing. He tells me about the decapitated body found in the trunk of a neighbor's car down the block. He's becoming worried about the Rouge River Killer again, but I assure him that the killer will eventually make a mistake and be caught. He's a sloppy bastard, Nick points out. You're probably right, he says.

May 1st, 8 AM. I've been shooting for three hours. I'm going to have to buy better quality arrows because I've already ruined 12. Archery is an expensive hobby. I'll need hunting arrows for the deer and the suburban cows. I'm still debating whether I want to pick them off with the bow or continue with my usual tools. The bow is like an early gun, the killing isn't intimate at all. It's like the point and click of a mouse. Still, I like the fantasy of a homicidal Robin Hood. Now that the weather has improved there will be more dog walkers and joggers on the streets. I could easily pick them off from my bedroom window. Taking a cow down with an axe or kukri is almost sexual, only better.

I go inside, packing up my bow and remaining arrows, and cook breakfast. I eat and take my pills with lukewarm black coffee. I like my coffee either cold or lukewarm. I used to joke that I like my coffee like I like my women: cold and bitter. I go online and look at hunting arrows. They're expensive. The arrowheads look like they could mangle anything. Deer, cow, doesn't matter to me. And since I already have the Ghillie suit I don't have to invest in camouflage. Deer hunting should be fairly straightforward once I'm skilled enough with the bow. I'll keep practicing every morning.

When Nick came today with the junk mail and asked how I was doing, I joked, Ain't dead yet. Now I'm carving gnomes for Dad in the basement with the radio on. I like to listen to classical when I'm carving; it helps me concentrate. I rough out three forms with the knife. I'll do the detail work later. I line the half-finished gnomes up in a row on the carving station table and go back upstairs.

I read a little bit of *Frankenstein*. I can relate to both characters; the ambitious, amoral creator and the monstrous creation. In high school it was my favorite novel. My memory has gotten so bad that I just reread the same books over and over again. I don't like contemporary fiction. I stick to the classics, back before the language became butchered. My biggest pet peeve is when the cows start a sentence with "Her and I." I'm not the grammar police but at least know the difference between a subject and an object. I guess not everyone went to Catholic school and received the same education. Either that or they're just lazy.

It's getting late which means it's time to go to work. There will be joggers out dressed in neon. Easy targets. I oil and sharpen the Damascus, lace up my killing boots, put on my coat and hat, head out the door.

The night is cool so I button my coat as I walk, the Damascus in its sheath hanging from my belt. The streets are empty and black; the street lights cast a long shadow beside me. I slink like a slithering snake down the sidewalks, walking in long strides like a stalking mountain lion. I walk past the high school and the cemetery, still no luck so I head down to the river. I walk the banks for twenty minutes until I hear a faint moaning sound coming from the bushes. I investigate and find two teenagers having sex. They're startled to see me but before they can dress themselves I make two deep slashes. In my disgust, I chop off the boy's dick and cram it into the girl's mouth, then sever her head. I leave them there to be eaten by rats. I cover their bodies in rocks and leaves beneath the dense bushes. They'll be found eventually if they aren't eaten first.

I stumble home in the darkness and vomit in the street. I vomit two more times before reaching home. Those kids got what they deserved. I probably prevented an abortion too. I go inside and lay down on the couch for a half hour, my mind reeling. I get up and clean my blade, take off my boots and outerwear. I go online and find Rose. I tell her what I saw and did and how I feel. You done good, she tells me. They shouldn't have been out past curfew anyway. And the bitch would have gotten pregnant so you probably saved them a lot of grief, she says. I begin to calm down.

The noises, the juices, the grotesque organs. It's so hideously disgusting to me. I've always felt this way; I don't know why. I only know that fornicating cows make me nauseous and I want them destroyed. I'll get to all that later. I still have to track down those art snobs. I go online and run a search. I remember their names, even though it was 22 years ago. The older one appears to be deceased, but the younger one, the head of the Illustration department, still lives in Detroit. I'll have to do some digging to find an address, but I have him now in my sights. I'll paint an abstract piece with his blood and brains.

The next morning, I shoot a few arrows and eat breakfast and wash down my pills with black coffee. I expect to hear from Saint Nick later about the Rouge River Killer's latest double homicide. Maybe they haven't discovered the bodies yet though. I hid them pretty well. The rats are hungry down by the river. I tidy up around the house and go downstairs to work on the gnomes. I define the facial features of each of them and start on the detail work of the clothing. It takes me two hours to finish all three. I place them on Dad's work desk and head back upstairs.

11:35 AM. Been leafing through my picture book of Egon Schiele's work. I don't know why I like it so much since it's so pornographic. I guess I just enjoy the way he rendered the figure; starved, emaciated, like posing mummies. There is death in his work and I enjoy that the most. He himself died of scarlet fever. Maybe I'll die of the virus and become famous as a suburban serial killer hermit artist. This is my hope. I'd rather become famous within my lifetime, but I'd rather not get caught. I have to keep working. Maybe someday my work will be recognized and I will be celebrated as the genius I am.

Saint Nick arrives late with more junk and news of the world. He tells me that two bodies were discovered at the river, one missing its head. The police are scrambling to find a suspect. The media is ablaze with panicked reports of The Rouge River Killer. The kids are making memes about him. I'm happy with what I've created. I've created a character who is famous; I'm still an unknown recluse but my creation is wildly popular. For now, that's good enough for me.

Jekyll created Hyde; Frankenstein, his Monster. Each inseparable from the other, just as I am both creator and creation. I take a sip of cold black coffee as I sit on the couch, absentmindedly whittling a stick I found outside. I'll clean up later. I'm compiling an online shopping list in my head. Soon I'll need arrows. I need to order toilet paper and cleaning products, and a few other odds and ends for around the house and yard. I'll have to start mowing the lawn again soon. I hate doing that. I don't like the stench of cut grass. I don't like being on the front lawn during the day, exposed. Maybe I'll just hire some neighborhood kid to do it. They don't have anything better to do with all the schools being closed. Might as well take advantage and be a job creator for some dumb, acne-ridden teenager.

4 PM. Time for psychotropic salad. I dump the pills out of their bottles and swallow them with cold, black coffee. I look

around the room. It's mostly clean aside from a little bit of clutter on the coffee table. I hope Mom would be happy that I keep the house tidy. I remember her each time I clean it. My eye is attracted to the mountain lion head once again, and I study it for a few minutes. It's not sanded and polished; you can see the chisel marks still, but I like it. Dad would have liked it too. He would have been proud of me. I'm proud of myself for all of my accomplishments over the last two months. I'm no longer killing time, I'm killing cattle.

For dinner I eat a steak then sit on the couch to watch a movie. *Lost in Translation*, another favorite. I whittle away at sticks from the yard making a mess of the coffee table. Mom would be pissed but I'll clean it up later. I'm debating whether to continue the random hits or start targeting individuals and groups. I'm still thinking about that art professor but I don't know how I'll get to him without my own car. I might have to pass on that job which is okay; I'm not much of a revenge killer, except for the priests. I loved how the old one started praying before I ruined his head. Heaven has no room for pedophiles, I don't think.

The Muslim community took the fall for the last killing. There's been building animosity between the white Christians and the Arab Muslims ever since 9/11. Then three Jesuit priests are murdered in their beds with what can only be described as a terrorist weapon. Jerry Mahone and his sideshow circus are back in town disrupting everything, preaching hate and retribution against Muslims both local and worldwide. Doesn't bother me though. Islam is just another religion meant to control the herd, and I have no more respect for it than I do Christianity. Let them kill each other. I could use a break.

I watch the local news at 11. The city's a mess. First the virus, then The Rouge River Killer, and now protests and increased hostility between Christians and Muslims within the community. I thrive on chaos. It gives me something to do. Maybe I should take out a few Muslims to place the blame back on the Christians then watch this thing really blow up. The media will blame Jerry Mahone and his flock which would be great. He might even be looking at prison time. Hopefully his cellmate is a Muslim who likes to cuddle.

7 AM, I'm showered and shaved. Nicked my scalp and bled all over the bathroom. Time for shooting practice. My bow is a beautiful piece of wood that is molded to fit my left hand. Lightweight too, which is important. I can't wait until I have

quality arrows. I only have a few left of the practice ones. I shoot for a few hours then go inside and eat eggs with black coffee. I pop pills. They're so colorful, so festive. I wonder if that is intentional by Big Pharma to cheer up us mental patients. I hate taking the pills but if I don't I'll lose control and be hospitalized again, and we can't have that. I sign on and talk to Rose for an hour. She and her boyfriend are quarantined in their house and are both working from home. I wonder what it's like in Iowa. All I imagine is cornfields like in *Field of Dreams*. Dad and I used to watch that movie together and cry at the end. I better not get into all of that or I'll just get sad. Dad's dead and it's my turn to take over the world.

I've been doing pretty well these last few weeks. I'm getting better at self-control and monitoring my mood swings. I haven't had crippling anxiety whenever I've left the house like I used to, and the killings have given me confidence in myself. Finally I can act out the fantasies without interruption. I think I'll Ghillie up and go sit down by the river. No mayhem, just calm meditation in nature. Maybe I'll watch the deer if they're out, and listen to the river birds. I suit up as Swamp Thing and begin the five block walk.

People look at me strangely as I walk, but I like the negative attention. I make my way to the woods where the river flows, sit down, and become one with my surroundings. No one is on the banks today, just me, and I'm a bush. I watch the dark water coursing through the riverbanks and imagine it to be blood. I don't see any rats, which is good because I loathe them. They're only good for cleaning up my messes. I spend about an hour sitting there when a deer appears. It's a doe with her calf, and they're just standing there minding their own business as I mind mine, unnoticed. I continue to watch them and feel the familiar prickling sensation on my skin whenever traces of empathy begin to enter my heart. I choke it down immediately. I'll be coming for them soon with my bow.

I walk back home still suited up in the Ghillie. Some little kids spot me and run. I pretend I'm a swamp monster. I can't wait for Halloween. I like giving out candy to the kids. I think that children are delightful little creatures. Too bad they grow up to be cows. I'll get them then, but for now I let them play. When I get home I go inside to the dimly lit living room. I change out of the suit and into my robe. It's late in the afternoon and I won't be leaving the house again today. I sit down on the couch and put on a movie. *I Heart Huckabees*, another favorite. I pick up the Damascus off the coffee table and practice slashing for a few minutes. I love that blade. It's brought me nothing but success and joy.

I cook a steak for dinner, then go online to shop for arrows. I quickly learn that they are expensive, so I won't be able to buy them in bulk like the practice arrows. I tell Rose about bow hunting the river and she erupts with happiness. She loves bow hunting and archery. It's funny to me that she's the man in her relationship, or at least she plays that stereotypical gender role. Her boyfriend is a computer dweeb whose only pastime is playing video games. I don't think they even have sex. None of my business though. I'm happy to have her in my life, even if it's virtual. Sometimes virtual is better than the real thing.

I purchase six top quality broadhead arrows for 50 bucks. I watch a few bow hunting videos on YouTube, then make my way over to the couch to sharpen my blades. I haven't taken the Plumb out in a while. I haven't used the dual kukris much either. I've been so in love with the Damascus that I've neglected my other friends. I'll have to take down a few randoms with them to keep my game up. I'm no slacker.

At midnight I go out with the two kukris. I'm feeling angry for no reason again. I just want to do damage. I hide behind a parked car a few blocks from my house and wait. As soon as I spot a jogger I leap out with my dual kukris flashing in the streetlight and make an utter mess of him. Nine slashes. I'm like a butcher. I don't know what to do with the slop of the body parts so I just leave them in the street and walk home. I feel better now. It's good to work out your aggressions doing productive, meaningful work. I wonder what the news will call me now. Saint Nick will tell me tomorrow.

The next day, I greet Saint Nick at the door. He tells me that the Rouge River Killer has struck again; this time in horrific fashion. Pieces of a body were found early this morning in the street not far from my house. It's all over the news, he says. I can tell he's nervous again, and I assure him that he'll be safe. I can't do rage killings anymore, I think to myself. It's sloppy and will only get me caught. I hope the arrows arrive soon; they'll make a quick, clean kill. I won't have to leave the house. I can pick them off one by one from my bedroom window.

I'm lying on the couch staring at the lion head again. I almost forgot about the Muslims. Going to have to take out at least a few to start up this holy war. Maybe next week I'll take a taxi to the east side of town. The cops don't police that area much so I'll be fine. They'll blame the murders on the Christian Trumper neo-Nazis and all hell will break loose. A religious war, a pandemic, a serial killer. Maybe these are the end times. I sharpen my kukris and mentally prepare myself. I'll work out the details tomorrow.

I decide to go with the Plumb instead. It will be easier to carry than two kukris, and it won't make as much of a mess. I figure I'll go for easy targets, the black-clad burka-wearing Muslim grandmothers that walk the sidewalks at all hours. Just one or two. That's all I'll need for my purpose. The trouble is getting in and out of there. I'll have to take a taxi, and that could pose problems, especially in getting back to the house. I just have to get to where all the Arabic restaurants are located, then knock a few of them on the head, and then lay low somewhere until the taxi arrives. It will be difficult, but if the result is jihad then it will be worth it.

I plan to do it next Tuesday. Today is Wednesday so I have time to think and prepare. The drive to the east side of town is only ten minutes without traffic, and there is no traffic anymore. I'm going to obsess over this for the next six days; maybe I should do it over the weekend so I don't become an anxious mess. There will be more cover then with the cows grazing the streets. I could easily knock one or two over the head unnoticed. I'll just have to get out quick. I can do this.

7 AM. I shoot the remaining practice arrows. I'm hitting the target now with greater accuracy. Soon I'll be hitting the bull's eye. I pop my pills and eat a quick breakfast of toast and orange juice, then go online. I order more practice arrows from eBay, then chat with Rose. You're going to start a holy war! she says. That's the plan, I say. If I can get the cows to kill each other, there will be no need for the Rouge River Killer, and I can retire without worry. But I do enjoy my work, and it's therapeutic. We'll see what happens. I'll wait for Saint Nick to give me the daily news.

1:45 PM. Saint Nick at the door with the usual junk. Have you heard the news? he asks me. Haven't been paying attention, I tell him. They're throwing rocks at each other, he says, the white Christians and the Muslims! Ever since the cathedral. This is crazy! he says. Could be worse, I say, quietly thinking that yes, indeed it will soon be worse. I change the subject and tell Nick that I'll be receiving a package tomorrow and he thanks me for the heads up. You work too hard, he says, you need to relax more. I chuckle and bid him farewell. Til tomorrow, I say.

I go sit on the toilet to reflect on my coming actions. I'd rather not take out Muslims but pawns must be sacrificed in order to win the game. Once both sides have suffered losses the real fun will begin. It will be chaos in the streets; I wonder if they'll call in the National Guard. I never planned to make history; at my most grandiose I imagined myself a famous serial killer artist with a cult following. But now I'll be remembered for much more. A new Crusade is about to begin; it already has, but now they'll be shooting each other. This city will become a slaughterhouse full of dead cows.

I spent the last couple days in meditation, calmly accepting the consequences of what I'm about to do. I feel righteous in my decision; the virus wasn't culling the herd fast enough. I'm just giving it a gentle nudge. Everything will be closed on the east side, the Lebanese restaurants and hookah bars, the juice shops and halal meat markets. It will just be me and the unfortunate few on the streets. I'll wear a surgical mask just in case, and dress in my casual Friday clothes, and carry a backpack with the Plumb inside it.

11:35 AM. I call a cab. After twenty minutes a white Dodge Ram pulls up in my driveway. I lock the doors, put on my coat, grab my pack. I get inside the truck. The driver is an old black man named Alphonse. We greet each other and chat for a little bit. He tells me that he was born in Jamaica and served in Nam, and has driven a cab ever since returning home. Saw some crazy shit over there, he says. People exploding, gang rape, everything. I saw a man fuck a pig then kill and eat it. Those were fucked up times, he says. I thank him for his service and he laughs. Fucked up times nowadays too, he says. That orangutan in office, telling people to inject themselves with bleach. It's madness, he says, and I nod in agreement. I tell him that if he parks the truck close to my destination then picks me up from the location I send him, I'll give him a hundred dollars under the table. I don't ask questions, he says. It's always better that way, I say.

After ten minutes of idle chat we reach Warren Avenue. I thank Alphonse and remind him to wait for my call. It won't take long, I say. I get out of the truck with my backpack and begin to walk. The truck pulls away and goes down the street. I pass Green Brain Comics and Detroit Jiu-JItsu, both empty. I continue to walk until I reach the old neighborhood where I grew up before we moved to the west side. I run across a couple black-shrouded old women and give them each a knock on the head. They drop into a black pool of tar. I have to get out of here now. I call Alphonse and he picks me up within minutes at the corner of the street. We don't talk on the drive home. Every so often I see him look at me in the rearview mirror. I hope he won't notice that my hands are shaking. When he pulls into my driveway he looks at me and says, I hope you got what you wanted. Oh yes, I say, oh yes.

When the mail comes at 2, Saint Nick gives me my package and looks at me horrified. Two more bodies, on the east side, he says. The Muslims are convinced it was Christian retaliation, and they've begun stockpiling guns and ammunition. When the Christians heard this, they raided the gun shops too. War is about to break out, Nick says. You'll be alright, I tell Nick. Just keep your family safe. Focus on your wife and girls, I say. Saint Nick thanks me and leaves. I go back inside.

Ah, the broadhead hunting arrows have arrived. I can hunt deer now, and eventually the moo cows. I touch the tip of the arrowhead and accidentally pierce the skin. I wash my finger in the bathroom and put a Band-Aid on it. The shafts are good and straight. These will do nicely. I only have 12 of them so

I'll have to retrieve them after every kill or I'll just be throwing away money. I think I'll go deer hunting this evening.

I try to keep busy so I don't think about the day's earlier events. I feel bad for killing those two women, but it had to be done. I put on some jazz and whittle a few sticks to keep my hands occupied. They're a little shaky. I don't know what's going to happen. America is still at war with the Middle East, and if news reaches ISIS they'll double their efforts against the U.S. I tend to look at it the same way I look at cleaning the house. The process is messy but when you're done everything is nice and neat and you can relax.

Evening comes so I suit up in the Ghillie and string my bow. I didn't think to buy a quiver so I take three arrows and carry them in my hand. I leave the house and make my way down to the river. I find a good, bushy spot, crouch down and disappear into the green and brown. I wait. I pop a lozenge. I wait some more. Soon a young buck appears across the river, approaches, and drinks. I rise with my bow, take aim at the heart, and fire. The buck flinches, then collapses, and I wade through the river to retrieve my arrow. The buck is still alive so I finish it with my knife. I remove my arrow and wash it in the river, saw off the antlers, then head home.

I'm washing the blood and slop off the rack. Removing it from the skull with just a knife was difficult, but I managed. It's illegal to hunt deer in the city, but laws are made by cows for cows. I finish up with the rack, go online, and learn how to make an antler crown. I'll just need a leather headband. I message Rose and ask her about it. She's crafty like that. She sends me a few online tutorials. I ask her how she's doing and she says she's incredibly bored, locked in the house with her boyfriend with little to do. She's played all her video games, read all her books, and doesn't feel like doing anything creative. I warn her not to become complacent, that she needs to exercise her artistic muscle unless she wants to lose it like I did. She says she'll start painting soon; right now she's just following the news. She asks me about what's going on in my town, that the news is reporting that people are throwing rocks at each other. They're about to start shooting guns, I tell her. I tell her what I did earlier today and she's shocked. Finally, Armageddon! she says.

The first shot was fired today at 4:45 PM, says the 6 o'clock news. A middle aged Muslim man armed with a glock shot an unarmed white man leaving the grocery store on the east side of town. It has begun, I think to myself. Fights are breaking out all over the city. The Christians are burning Korans and the Muslims are burning Bibles. Jerry Mahone has responded with more Islamophobia rhetoric, which has fueled the young neo Nazis, who are taking to the gun ranges. Soon everything will be chaos. The dead cows slaughtered in the streets. They're doing the work for me. They're doing it to themselves. Soon they'll all be gone, and nature will reclaim this land. Soon, everything will be green again, and I can finally be at peace.

I grill a steak in the backyard and listen to the gunshots. I'll get the latest from Saint Nick tomorrow afternoon. I can already hear the carnage. The cows wet with blood, their tongues lolling out of their mouths. Flesh riddled with bullet holes. It's all coming together. And all of it because of me. Who would have thought a few dead priests would launch an all-out war. I didn't expect it at the time I killed them, but I'm happy with the result. I just have to stay inside for a while until this blows over. I'm supposed to be staying inside anyway. The virus still spreads, but now everyone is distracted by the war in southeastern Michigan. I wonder if it will spread to other states, or even countries? Have I started the third World War? That's silly, they'll call in the National Guard eventually and put this thing down quick. I may be a killer and a misanthrope but I don't want to be the last man alive on the planet. Then there'd be no one to kill.

At 1 PM the next day Saint Nick is frantic on my front porch. It's anarchy! he tells me. They're shooting each other and looting stores! Police and ambulances are everywhere! Haven't you watched the news? I heard the gunshots, I tell him. I knew this day would come eventually. I express concern for his safety and he says he's concerned too, but he can't afford to quit his job. I have no marketable skills, he says. I'm a rocker; I either rock or deliver mail. Not much else I'm any good at, he says. I take the junk and wish him luck, then throw the junk into the garbage.

All the Muslims moved here back in Ford's day when he opened the assembly lines and there were jobs for everyone. The resentment started then. It escalated in the early 90's during the Gulf War, then 9/11 came and that was it. Blatant acts of bigotry all over town for the past two decades. And now this. I remember growing up on the east side and being bullied and made fun of by the Arabic kids. Even then the white and Arabic kids hated each other. And all the adults were either secretly or openly racist. I lived in a mixed neighborhood with my parents where there was always tension under the surface. All the whites have since moved to the west side of town, and the east side is almost entirely Muslim. Now they're shooting each other, and I'm responsible. The Christians and the Muslims have been slaughtering each other for thousands of years. I just stoked the fire.

Just to clarify: I hate Christians and Muslims equally. Both religions are built upon fairy tales about beings that don't exist. So I'm not a Nazi or a hatemonger. I'm a killer, a ringleader, a puppeteer. When I pull the strings the puppets get busy, and that pleases me. The grandest circus is already beginning, and I get to watch it from the comfort of my own home. I watch the carnage out the front window, sitting in my dad's old chair, eating sunflower seeds. They've forgotten about the Rouge River Killer. Now everyone's a killer, and someday, someone will trace this back to me. Probably not in my lifetime though. It's sad; I'd like to be famous and remembered, but my deeds might go unrecognized and unappreciated, like my other creative work.

I take a shower, ice cold, and cleanse my body of all the grunge. I'm going to run out of soap and it's unsafe to go outside so I don't know what I'm going to do. I suppose I could order soap online. I feel bad for Saint Nick and the other mail carriers. They're sitting ducks out there. I need my packages though. I care about Saint Nick but he can be replaced. These days you gotta look out for number one and that's it.

7 PM. It's been a long day. You can still hear sirens and gunshots in the distance. I haven't watched the news. I wonder if I'm becoming grandiose again. Maybe the police will contain it. I don't know if they're going to try to take on the police, but if they do, it's going to be a national emergency. I'll talk to Nick tomorrow. Right now I'm fiddling with a leather strap I ordered, trying to figure out how I could make it into an antler crown. Maybe I'll just mount the antlers on the wall next to the mountain lion head. I should be carving. Dad would be disappointed that I'm not. I've been busy though. Now that we're on double lockdown I should start another big project. I know. I'll carve a mount for the antlers. It will be boring work but challenging, and challenging is good. Never stop climbing the mountain. Once you reach the top, climb back down and do it all over again.

10 PM and I'm lying on the couch, staring into empty space. When I lived alone the walls were bare and I liked it that way. I love staring at bare walls. It's a good way to meditate. It is

said that one Buddhist monk stared at the same wall for nine years. I strive to be like him. The artwork I created was never intended to be used as decoration or for a gallery. Painting was my therapy, and I slashed the canvas with the large brush in broad strokes. After art school, I stopped painting, and moved on to other things.

At midnight I climb in bed and think my thoughts for a few hours before passing out. I sleep a dreamless sleep and wake refreshed the next morning. Today must be Sunday. I wonder if all the mayhem is still going on. I look out the window and don't see anything out of the ordinary, so I assume I'm safe. I go online and watch bow hunting videos, then chat with Rose for a bit. She's doing better. She's painting again. She sends me pictures of her paintings and they're very good. Maybe when I retire from all this I'll take up painting again. Then Rose and I can paint together. That would be nice.

She asks me about the crisis going down in my city, and I tell her the media exaggerates everything. I don't want her to worry about me. Apparently this thing is getting national coverage, and riots have broken out in other cities across the country. Jerry Mahone is being heralded as the next Messiah. If he comes back to town, they're going to eat him alive. I tell

Rose that I'll be safe. I'll do some carving until it all blows over, I tell her, which is the truth. I tell her about the antlers I found and how I'm going to carve a wall mount for them. She becomes excited. She's so encouraging. That's one of the reasons why I love her so much.

I'm taking a piss and thinking my thoughts. I shouldn't have used the Muslims as scapegoats for my crimes. Maybe I can help them out a bit since I fucked them over so hard. Maybe I can serve my penance by hunting neo Nazis. I've always disliked them a great deal, but believed that you had to tolerate even the intolerant. I don't believe that anymore. Those Nazi punks are idiots, and they've just been waiting for an excuse to commit genocide in this town. Not on my watch. They won't suspect me because I'm white, but when they feel the heft of my axe they'll know who I am.

I spend the rest of the day watching the news. The new crisis is national in scope and spreading to other countries. They're tracing it back to southeastern Michigan. Christians and Muslims are at each other's throats, and now they're using bombs. I had no idea. I thought Saint Nick was freaking out over nothing, but apparently I was wrong. For the Christians, it's the New Crusade; for Muslims, the New Jihad. Those three dead priests were the first three dominos, and now they're all knocking each other down. I'll go to work tonight.

6 PM and I'm all suited up. Camo balaclava, black pea coat. My kukris are sharp and oiled and hungry for Nazi flesh and bone. I call up Alphonse and tell him same deal as last time. He says no problem and hangs up. He's in my driveway in ten minutes. You look like you're going to war, he says. I am, I say, it's Nazi season. He laughs and calls me a crazy white boy. I tell him he has no idea. Warren Avenue is a warzone. People are running and screaming and shooting, just like in my dreams. I tell Alphonse to be ready for my call. No worries, chief, he says.

I stay on the fringes and bide my time. A neo Nazi with a shaved head and a swastika tattoo on his shoulder runs past me, and I turn around and slash him in the back of the neck. He goes down. I walk over to him, pick up his head in my hand and slice his throat with the kukri. I continue in this fashion for the next 15 minutes, taking down three other Nazis, then I call Alphonse. Get me outta here, I say. Sure thing, boss. Be right over, Alphonse says. I return to where I was dropped off, and Alphonse pulls up looking concerned. My kukris are dripping, red and wet. He doesn't ask questions. I hand him the hundred cash and he drives me home. When we arrive at the house, I tell him I'll be in touch. He nods and drives on.

I go inside and wipe my kukris clean. Nazi blood. Disgusting. I take the balaclava off, and my pea coat, and settle in for the night. No one will know that I killed those punks, but they're dead now and so that's good. I'll go back out tomorrow night. I watch a movie then the 11 o'clock news. More carnage, more virus, mass hysteria. I'm surprised that I've remained relatively calm throughout all this. The klonopin must be working; otherwise, I'd be an anxious mess like poor Saint Nick. I hope he's doing okay. I take out the Damascus and oil the blade. At least the Rouge River Killer is off the news. I was fixing to get myself caught with my last few slop messes. Now I have a righteous mission. I'm the hero, a Nazi hunter, and this is no video game.

The police are racist just like the neo Nazis, so my side of town is pretty safe. The Muslims haven't attacked the white people on the west side; it's the Nazis who have gone to the east side of town who have stirred up all the trouble. So I'll have to go to them. I have Alphonse to get me there. I'll go back out in a couple nights. I need a break. I need to carve the mount for the antlers so I'm watching carving videos, trying to figure out how to do it without power tools. Dad preferred traditional hand carving.

The next day, I decide not to carve the mount. I would need power tools, so I need a new idea. Maybe I'll carve another mountain lion. Or another animal. I've always liked badgers; maybe a nice, snarling badger head would be fun. Yes, I think I'll do that. I get photo reference off the internet and go downstairs to the basement. I take a large block off the shelf, pick up the knife, and start roughing out the form. In two hours it looks somewhat badger-like. I'll have to spend time with it. Carving is good for my patience. It's calming and gives me a sense of accomplishment, but it also takes time. I have nothing but time. That's my own personal superpower.

The badger head is coming along nicely. I've worked on it throughout the day, and the form is complete. Now I'm starting the detail work, the tedious part. I take many breaks but by the end of the day the head is mostly done, just have to define the fur more with fine cuts. It's much smaller than the mountain lion head, which is why I finished so quickly, but I like it nearly as much. I've decided to carve a golden eagle next.

Time to shit and think my thoughts. Looking back on it, my career as the Rouge River Killer was all a warm up to what I'm doing now. I'm not killing random dumb cows; now, my enemy is much more calculating, a much more worthy adversary. I'll have to find out if the Nazis have a website and maybe infiltrate their ranks. It would be incredibly risky, but possible. I'll cut down any white skinhead I see in town, but I'm really after the ringleader.

I still think of people as cows, but the Nazis are another creature entirely. They're methodical and cunning, like me. I don't believe in rounding people up and exterminating them though. I had my fun with taking down the cows I did, but now things are getting serious. I'm staring down a fellow mountain lion, so I can't be reckless. I have to be cold, take them out like vermin. Serial killing was getting old and boring anyway. There was no purpose behind it except to exorcize my own demons. Now I'm a hunter. I know my prey. I will be coming for them soon.

I spend the evening on the couch, watching *The Maxx* animated show from back when MTV was worth watching. I make the realization that Rose is my virtual Jungle Queen. That makes me chuckle. I pop a lozenge and go online. Rose is active so I chat her up. I tell her that she's my Jungle Queen and she laughs, saying, Damn straight! I tell her about my plan to take out the neo Nazis. She applauds my decision. She says I've finally found my calling, that I'm not a heartless serial killer, I'm an agent of justice. I laugh and tell her that she can think of me however she wants.

6 AM. Shower, shave, shit. Eat pills. Brush teeth. Put on robe and go downstairs. My sleep has improved. I'm getting back on a regular schedule again. I haven't been moody or anxious; my newfound purpose has given me clarity and focus. Maybe I'm not a monster. Or maybe, I'm the monster that eats bad guys. I've noticed that more and more of the young white men in the neighborhood have taken to shaving their heads. Lots of Viking imagery on their t-shirts too. They're in the neighborhood. That is spectacular. I won't have to cross town anymore, not for a while at least. That's good because I can't afford to keep paying Alphonse off for his silence.

I put the finishing touches on the badger head and go out into the backyard for target practice. With these dipshits walking past my house, I can just pick them off from my bedroom window. I'll still go for my walks too. This is going to be fun.

It's like a real life video game, a first person shooter. I'm going to have to stock up on arrows. It will be worth the expense

I drink black coffee in my dad's chair and look out the window. I do this for an hour, and notice two young white men with shaved heads, boots, and braces walking past my house. Maybe a little later I'll see if I can catch up with them. Right now I'm relaxing. I should go online to see if I can find their website. Maybe there's a local group on social media. I wish I was a hacker so I could disrupt their communications somehow, if that is even possible. I guess I'll just have to do it the old-fashioned way.

I go online and run a search for hate groups in the area, but no luck. It was stupid of me to think they'd have an online public presence. I'll ask Saint Nick where these skinheads are coming from. Once I know the location of their nest, it will be like shooting fish in a barrel. The way the dumbasses strut around in their jack boots like grotesque cartoons, they'll be easy targets for my arrows. If only I could locate the head of the operation. I have time.

I'm standing at my open bedroom window that looks out onto the street, bow and arrows at the ready. One of the Nazi weasels comes strutting down the sidewalk. I aim for his neck, and fire. He drops instantly. I run downstairs and out the door to retrieve my arrow, and drag the body down the basement. I saw off the head and limbs. I carve a swastika into his forehead. Six chunks in black bags. I'll haul them to the river tonight. I go back to my bedroom window. Two more skinheads, two more arrows. Soon, more chunks in garbage bags, for a total of 18 bags. It will take me a few nights to get all these down to the river, and I should probably only take out one at a time so my basement isn't overflowing with body parts. It feels good to be doing good.

Saint Nick arrives at 3 and apologizes for his tardiness. I ask him if he's noticed the skinheads in the neighborhood, and he tells me that a group of them bought a house a few blocks down. Fuck racism, he says. It's all-out war on the east side, he says, the cops can't keep up. They're shooting each other in the streets, he says. He gives me the Nazis' address and I thank him. More junk mail, more packages of arrows. I tell him to keep his chin up and that this will all be over soon. He says he's not too worried; the Nazis wouldn't shoot a white mailman, but he's concerned for the Muslims across town. I tell him not to worry about them. Soon they'll be safe again and the city will go back to its quiet racism.

I sit on the couch and open the packages of arrows. Good quality, straight and true. The archery practice paid off; I'm now skilled with the bow, like when I was a boy scout. I now have about 40 arrows, and if I keep retrieving and reusing them, I should have more than enough ammunition. I should go for a walk tonight with the Plumb or the Damascus. I need to figure out a better way of getting the bodies down to the river. Carrying them in dad's wheelbarrow could get me caught, and the river is five blocks away. I wonder if I paid off Alphonse again if he'd allow me to do the transport in the bed of his Ram. It would be a risky request, but so far he's kept his mouth shut. I'll call him later.

I go for a walk, armed only with my pocket knife. I'm not hunting this time; this is an information gathering mission. The neo Nazi house is four blocks north of my own. I stroll through the neighborhood under a blue sky, sun shining. When I pass the house, three skinheads are sitting in rocking chairs on the front porch. I wave at them but they don't wave back. I wonder how many of the rats are living in there. It's a large house, so I'm thinking four or five Nazis. If they keep walking around the neighborhood openly displaying their hatred, this is going to be easy. I wonder if their leader is living in the same house.

I walk back home. I'd rather take them out at their house because they live a block up from the river, but that would be too dangerous. They have guns and outnumber me. I may be a one man army but I'm not invincible. I'll pick them off one at a time with my bow and blades. Like the good old days. At least they're easy to spot with their skinhead costumes on. There are probably many Nazi sympathizers in the neighborhood, especially after the cathedral killings. But those dumb, passive cows don't have the balls to take to the streets like these young bucks. There are many more of them downtown in the city. But I'm not taking that risk. I just want them out of my neighborhood.

I reach my front door and go inside. I need to rest. My mind has been racing with plots and schemes to exterminate the vermin I now must call my neighbors. I go online and chat with Rose about the current situation. You might want to take out a few of those jihadists too, she says. They're equally at fault, she says. I think they're just defending their territory. I don't want to kill any more Muslims. I started this war and I have to end it. I miss the days of killing randoms in the streets. Things were so uncomplicated then. Now I've started to question my actions and blame myself for all the mayhem

I've caused. I hope I'm not developing a conscience. That would be bad for business.

10 PM. I call Alphonse. I tell him I'll pay him 200 dollars if I can transport some garbage in his truck. He agrees and says he'll be there in 20 minutes. I carry the bags up from the basement and set them by the front door. I'm not going to be able to fit all 18 bags in his truck, but I can fit most of them. The remaining few I'll take to the river myself with Dad's wheelbarrow. At 10:30 Alphonse pulls up. I carry 12 bags out to his truck, one by one, and place them carefully in the bed. Maybe he'll make two trips. No problem, Alphonse says when I ask. He doesn't ask questions, just drives us the five blocks to the river. I get out and haul the bags to the edge of the bank and dump them in the black water. I get back in the cab and Alphonse says, Doing a little spring cleaning, huh? I smile and nod yes. We drive back to my house to pick up the six remaining bags, then I dump them in the river like before. You're a hard worker, says Alphonse. You're doing good work, he says with a wink. I wish him a good night when we return home, hand him the 200 cash, and go inside to the darkness.

6 AM. I wake up but stay in bed. Today is a rest day. After hauling those bags around last night I'm physically exhausted.

After 20 minutes of staring at the ceiling, I get up and put my robe on. I go through my morning routine, trying to think of something productive to do with the day. I could start carving the golden eagle. Or I could go online and dick around and look at antique weapons and talk to Rose. The eagle can wait, I'm too tired for that today. I'm just going to lay on the couch and watch movies and listen to music, maybe some reggae or ska. Haven't listened to any of that in a while. I put on The Specials and lay down on the couch while "A Message to You, Rudy" plays. I want to listen to The Clash next. I should order another copy of *London Calling* since my copy skips from all the listens I've given it over the years. I lay on the couch, lost in thought. I try to pay attention to the music but I can't. I shouldn't be thinking about work on my day off, so I get up and put on The Clash and cook breakfast.

At 11 I sit down and watch episodes of *Northern Exposure* on one of the streaming channels. It's my favorite show. I love all the characters and the scenery. I'd like to live in a small town like that, way up north. Not in this godforsaken suburb. I'm getting tired of all the conservative politics; the racism, the sexism, the homophobia, all the neo Nazi Republican shit. I know the Muslims aren't special but I have more sympathy for them and their plight than I do for these suburban rednecks. Too dumb to know their days are numbered.

At 1:35 Saint Nick arrives with the usual junk. He tells me about the religious conflict and how things have settled down a bit, though someone did throw a rock through one of the cathedral windows. Wasn't me, I say. We laugh. He seems more relaxed today and I'm glad for that. I ask him about his family and he says they're doing fine, though it's difficult keeping the girls occupied with the schools still closed. I tell him they should all become woodcarvers like me. Nick says he'd love to see more of my work sometime, and I tell him about the big golden eagle project I'm planning. That will be awesome, he says, and departs.

I blare Metallica's black album and bang my head for a while. "Unforgiven" is my favorite song on the album, and I love the music video. It used to scare me as a kid. I've found that most of the things that frightened me as a child now intrigue me, like weapons and killers and all the bloody stuff. I was a sensitive boy. Mom took care of me and I would wrestle with Dad in the evenings when he got home from work. I allow myself to remember for a few minutes, then I go online and talk to Rose. Iowa is on lockdown so she can't send me anything in the mail. She was planning on sending me her Icelandic sheepskin as a gift but now she can't and she's upset. I talk to her until she's comforted. She tells me that she loves me and that we'll talk more often again soon. I miss her.

I'm actually starting to feel lonely; I haven't felt that way in years. Everyone is imprisoned in their homes, all non-essential businesses are closed. The governor put us on lockdown yesterday. I wonder if depression is creeping back into my head. I don't feel motivated to hunt like I did before. It'll pass, I tell myself. It always does. I wish Mom were here to comfort me. She would rub my head and tell me that everything is going to be okay. I miss Dad too. I miss smoking cigars with him and drinking beer on the back patio back before any of this mess began.

I remember Christmas 1992. I was 12 and Mom and Dad bought me the Super Nintendo. The tree was strung with cranberries and popcorn with all our ornaments hanging from the branches. The little old wooden man riding his sled, the cuckoo clock, the miniature bookcase in the shape of a tree. Mom and Dad smiling and laughing as I ripped open my presents with abandon. Would they be disgusted and ashamed of me now? Most likely. But they'd still love me. I know they would.

I turn the lights on. Maybe that will put me in a better mood. Surely sitting in the dark won't help. I agonize over a haiku before abandoning it. I should really get to work on the eagle but I just don't feel right. Maybe all the killing has finally caught up with me. Maybe I'm thinking too much. I go online and look at vintage hatchets on Etsy. I chat with my virtual girlfriends and make sure they're all alright. Then I sharpen my blades and rub them with gun oil. Eat a sandwich. Everyone is posting about having cabin fever and I laugh. I've had cabin fever for decades.

I'm cracking my knuckles on the couch. I pop a lozenge, then take my afternoon dose. I need to call the doctor soon but I think his office must be closed. I don't know if psychiatric clinics are considered essential businesses. I will be needing refills soon. If I run out I don't know what the fuck I'm going to do. Probably get arrested. I spent a night in jail once. I was psychotic and attacked a classmate in broad daylight. Lucky for me there were no real consequences. The doctor just adjusted the medications and I was fine. And the classmate eventually forgave me, so it was like nothing happened.

Now I'm flossing my teeth out of boredom. I finish and go back to the living room. I'm starting to feel like a caged animal. I want to ruin someone's day. It's my day off but the urges are strong. Maybe I'll go for a walk later and see what I can see.

7 PM. I cook a steak, eat it, shit it back out. I could watch another movie to pass the time. Maybe *Apocalypse Now*. That would be fitting for the times. I put it on and watch for a half hour, then begin to lose focus. I blare OutKast while the film plays. I like having lots of stimulation. Chaos. It's what keeps life moving. I've often thought that good and evil are fantastical constructs of society; that the dichotomy is really order and chaos, with a broad spectrum in between opposite extremes. I've brought chaos to my community, and though I feel no personal responsibility to restore order, I enjoy killing Nazis, so that's what I'll do.

The next morning I rise early and get ready for the day. I'm going Nazi hunting today. I practice target shooting with the bow for a few hours, but I won't be needing it later. It's time to take out the Damascus. I sharpen and oil the blade so it'll be ready for my walk. I'll wait until dusk. In the meantime, I can start the golden eagle. It won't be as large as I wish it could be.

I'm running out of large blocks of bass wood and I have ideas for other larger projects. I go down to the carving station in the basement and get to work, taking off large strips of wood with my knife, shaping the wood into an eagle. This takes several hours and I manage to cut myself twice; battle scars, Dad always said.

Saint Nick knocks at the door at 2. More catalogues. My phone and internet bills. Nick tells me that a mosque on the east side of town was burned to the ground last night. The police have no suspects, but I know it's those rotten bastards a few blocks down, or their kin. I assure him that everything will be alright and that he won't be targeted. He nervously smiles and heads back out. I throw the catalogues in the trash and think my thoughts. Those dipshits burned down a mosque. Luckily it was closed due to the virus so no one got hurt, but still, it's a hate crime in what will surely become a series of hate crimes on both sides.

Three hours later I suit up and leave the house, the Damascus in its sheath. I walk for several blocks under the streetlights, taking notice of the flowers blooming. Mom would have liked to see them. Tulips were her favorite. A few minutes later a drunken skinhead comes into view, headed my way down the sidewalk. Easy peasy, I say to myself. He comes within striking distance and pushes me out of his way, and in one fluid motion I unsheathe the Damascus and slash, sending his head rolling down the sidewalk, leaving a trail of red in its wake. I continue on my walk toward the Nazi house. A party is underway. The neo Nazis are smoking and drinking on the large front porch, going in and coming out. A female skin walks to the side of the house to hit her crack pipe. I follow her, ask her for a hit, then plunge the Damascus into her guts, twisting the blade until her eyes roll back in her head. I make a hasty exit. Good thing the Nazis were too drunk and drugged to notice me.

Two hits in one night, that's not too bad, I say to myself on the walk home. Plenty more work to be done, though. I'll take out the bow tomorrow and pick off a few more with any luck. Back at my house, all the lights are still on and I curse myself for wasting electricity. Gonna have a big, fat bill this month, then I head over to the couch. If these fools like to party, this is going to be easy. I just can't be seen. I bet Warren Ave. is a hot mess right now, after the burning of that mosque. The idiots were probably celebrating. Justice, bloodlust, psychosis, call it what you will. It's all the same thing to me.

The next day, 2:44 PM. Nick's at the door with more bills and catalogues. He tells me about the killing at the Nazi house and how police are investigating. They found another body with its head sliced clean off on the sidewalk not far from here, and they think it's all the work of the Rouge River Killer. Or the Muslims. They don't quite know since there is no evidence at this time. And there never will be. I cover my tracks well and wear gloves to hide my fingerprints. Still, Nick says, the Nazis are retaliating. They're going into the neighborhoods on the east side and opening fire with AR-15's. The police are scrambling to make arrests, but they're understaffed and stretched to the limit. Many of them have contracted the virus and are quarantined. It's a field day for killers of all stripes. I've created a murderer's paradise, and much work needs to be done before I hang up the hatchet.

6 PM and I'm shaving my head. I lather up the cream and apply it liberally to my scalp and neck. I take the razor and begin to shave, with long, delicate strokes. Once I finish I splash my head with water and dry off, then put my shirt back on. It's a chore but I don't trust a barber to do it. I've let my beard grow long again out of sheer laziness; I haven't had the need to look professional and I've been mostly indoors along

with everyone else. I look like a mad hermit. I suppose that's accurate.

I lay on the couch and think my thoughts. I thought there were at most five or six Nazis in the neighborhood, but there was a horde of them at that house the other night. I don't know if they all live in town or not, but I have more work cut out for me than I originally imagined. I wish I could recruit the neighborhood youth and build a teenaged army to take out these goons. Fanciful thinking will get me nowhere, I remind myself. I'm just going to have to pick them off one by one. It's going to take time and patience. I have the first but I lack the latter.

I stare at the walls for twenty minutes thinking, then pick up the Damascus from the coffee table to inspect it. I've done a good job keeping it cleaned, sharpened, and oiled. I take care of my tools. It's quickly becoming my favorite method of dispatch, though I still love my Plumb. The Damascus is more versatile though, lighter too. One slash, instant kill. I like that. I hope I get the opportunity to use the twin kukris again. I still practice with them when nothing else is going on, along with target shooting with the bow. I'm slowly becoming skilled in the use of a variety of weapons, and that gives me a sense of confidence and pride.

8 PM and I'm chipping away at the golden eagle, defining talon, beak, and feather with my little blade. When I'm carving I'm able to focus and concentrate, and my thoughts don't wander off like they have a tendency to do when I'm idle. Not that I don't love being idle, it's just nice to be crafty and precise now and again. The eagle should be finished within a few days, then I'll place it on the mantle along with the badger and mountain lion head. Rose tells me that I should sell my work on Etsy, but I grow too attached to it. I can't put a price tag on my creations. They're for me alone. The thought of some stranger displaying my work in their home is revolting to me.

Midnight. I'm lying on the couch half asleep when I get an alert on my phone. The Governor put the state on lockdown effective immediately. I've been through this before, back when Mom and Dad died two years ago, when the first outbreak occurred. I'll have to stay indoors and only leave for groceries and pills. The Nazi killing will have to be postponed for now. Hopefully they contract the virus and save me some work.

6 AM. Morning ritual but I skip the shower and shave out of not giving a shit today. I listen to the radio and it says that we're still allowed to go outside and walk and exercise, go to the grocery store and pharmacy, but otherwise we're stuck at home. This doesn't change my life much, and I'll be able to still go out and work. The Nazis will probably be partying most of the time, so I can make my hits when they're fucked up on their booze and drugs. I'm doing their neighbors a favor.

I go downstairs and cook breakfast. Eggs and sausage. I eat while doodling on a piece of scrap paper. It's an abstract piece I'm calling "March of the Shit Robots." I put some music on and sit on the couch. The Pogues' *Rum, Sodomy, and the Lash*. Good stuff. I've got a bit of Irish in me, or at least that's what Dad always told me. My ancestors are from all over Europe. I don't get big into genealogy. I don't care if I'm the descendant of kings. I'd rather be descended from Viking berserkers, but I doubt that I am. I need a Viking axe. Maybe I'll do some online shopping later today.

Rose is online and she's thrilled that I'm taking out neo Nazis. Slaughter those racist pieces of shit! she says. I chuckle at her enthusiasm. I think I'm addicted to it. She gives me an update on her status. She and the boyfriend have been playing a lot of video games. But she's painting again too, which is good. She's using oils now instead of acrylics and is very pleased with the results. She sends me a photo of a landscape she painted and it's incredible. You should really go pro, I tell her, but she's self-conscious about her work. She hasn't sold anything lately in her Etsy store and is feeling discouraged. She could really use the money right now, she says. I try to encourage her but her mood has changed. I'll check up on her again later today.

I run a search for Viking axes on eBay and find a bunch of cheap LARP junk. After a few minutes I find the one. A brand new, Norse bearded axe, exactly the kind I'm looking for. There's a minute left on the auction. The current bid is 31 dollars, so I put in my maximum of 50 and nervously wait. The bids increase a few dollars at a time, then the auction is over and the axe is mine, for only 40 bucks. I'm excited. I'm going to hang it on the wall next to my wooden sculptures. I might even use it in my work.

I go downstairs and chip away at the eagle for a few hours. The head is mostly finished and now I'm doing the tedious detail work defining each feather. Dad would be proud of me. The sculpture is about 12 inches tall, so it's not massive, but it's a comfortable size to work with. After I've had enough, I head back upstairs and sit on the couch, pop a lozenge, and read the latest issue of *Heavy Metal*. My axe should be arriving in about a week. I relish the thought of taking out these pseudo-Norse heathen Nazis with a Viking axe. Poetic justice.

2 PM. Saint Nick arrives with the garbage. Nothing exciting. But he has news. Apparently someone threw rocks through the stained glass windows of the cathedral and the cops suspect it was the work of the Muslims. It could have been anybody. The neo Nazis will be up in arms. Nick says Warren Avenue is still a mess. Both sides have broken into businesses and are shooting at each other from the windows. Soon they'll be out of ammo, I think to myself. Then things are going to get messy.

Starting to miss Mom and Dad again. I allow myself a few minutes to indulge in the pain. I remember working with Dad on the house when I was a teenager. We built the backyard patio together one summer. Mom would bring us lemonade and sandwiches. Those were idyllic times. Now everything is plague and war. I embrace the chaos, but sometimes I miss the stability of their presence. They gave me structure and love. I don't feel much love anymore. I wonder what Mom and Dad would think of me now. Surely they'd be horrified. I ponder that thought for a few seconds then shift my attention to my blades. I sharpen and oil them and try to forget.

I lay on the couch for the next hour, staring at the mountain lion head. I have to keep focused on the task before me. I don't have time for silly thoughts of the past. That life is over; it died when Mom and Dad did. I'm a predator now. I've found my perfect prey. I know they're not all boozers and drug addicts. There has to be someone who's pulling the strings. Someone smart and cunning. He's my ultimate target. Then maybe this charade can be over. I just have to find out who and where. I'll continue to take out the cubs until they're gone from my neighborhood, but the big hit is going to be that other lion.

6 PM. I went out for a walk and took down one cub down at the river. I dragged him beneath the tall grasses and rocks. I'm sure the Nazis are aware that someone is picking off their members, but they probably blame the Muslims. Now I'm back inside in Dad's chair, looking out the front window. Not many cars on the roads these days. Not many people walking either. I wonder if it's going to get worse. The virus and the

holy war are decimating the city; it's the silence of the cows. I would just hang up the hatchet if it weren't for the Nazi menace.

I slept for three hours and woke at 5 AM. My dreams were disturbing; I saw Mom and Dad, only they were monsters chasing me through a forest. It didn't make any sense but it scared me. I'm not easily scared and am glad to be awake now. I go on the computer. I'm trying to find information on the neo Nazis. I'm surprised to find that their national headquarters is right here in Detroit, and their leader is a man named Bradley Wilson. Of course it doesn't give his location, but I can do some digging, and ask Rose for help. She's a computer genius who can track down anything. I send her a message and she instantly replies. Glad to help! she says.

I decide to not go for a walk and focus on research today with the help of Rose. She soon infiltrates their online ranks by becoming a member of the National Socialist Movement, centered in Detroit. She knows what she's doing so I don't question her. She subscribes to all the online newsletters and joins Nazi groups and chats with the vermin in their chatrooms. She's a great actress and was born to play this role. German, blonde haired, blue eyed daughter of the fatherland.

This is perfect. Soon she gathers a bunch of information about the movement, its members, and even locates Bradley Wilson, all within hours. Apparently he lives in Westland, a neighboring suburb. He's old and lives alone. He's a recluse like me, and his followers bring him everything he needs. He just spews hatred from his home through writing and video. He doesn't even leave the house. I'm sure the house is well guarded by his minions, so this will take some time to plan out. I thank Rose for her performance and she says she'll keep an eye on their activities and continue spying on them. We'll fuck them up good, she says.

When Saint Nick knocks at the door I open it with enthusiasm. I ask him if he can get an address for me in Westland. Nick looks confused but says that he has friends who carry mail in Westland, that he'll find the address. We talk about the neo Nazis who moved in down the street and Nick says he wants them dead and gone. If only the Rouge River Killer were still around, he says, he'd take care of them. I tell him not to worry, that they won't be around for long. Nick gives me a funny look and smiles. We say goodbye after he hands me the usual junk.

Several days go by uneventfully, then one Wednesday afternoon Nick knocks at the door. He's holding a long package. He hands it to me immediately and says he has good news. I had to call in some favors, he says, but I got that address you wanted. He hands me a scrap of paper with numbers and words written on it. I thank him kindly and he doesn't ask any questions, just smiles and says, Happy to help. See ya tomorrow! I close the front door. I take the package to the couch and open it. Inside under the brown paper wrapping and bubble tape is a work of art, a Norse bearded axe. This thing is too pretty to kill with, I say to myself. Then again, I've killed with the Damascus, and that bad boy is beautiful.

I go online and search Google maps for the address. I find it in an instant. Too easy, I say to myself. I'll have to give Saint Nick a bonus this Christmas. I message Rose and tell her I have the Wilson address. She's overjoyed. She tells me that she struck up an online romance with one of the bastards in Detroit, one of the top guys. He wants her to come visit him and she tells me that she has a plan. She'll drive her truck to Michigan and stay with me, go on a few fake dates with the Nazi until she's earned his trust, then ask to meet Wilson. I want to kill him myself, she says, Fuck the virus.

I'm flabbergasted. Rose is coming to Detroit and is going to kill the head of the National Socialists? This is too great for me to express in words. She says she's planned it all out; she's stocked up on food and supplies and has everything she needs. She'll head out in a few days. Her boyfriend will survive. She says this is important to her and that it's high time we met. She too wants to accomplish something great in her lifetime. I'm not going to stop her. She has guns and poisons and is skilled with both. I just have to wait for her arrival. It's going to be a long few days.

I go downstairs to the carving station and work on the feathers for a few hours. Could this actually work, or am I putting Rose in harm's way? It's extremely dangerous for either of us, but she seems hellbent on getting it done herself. She inspires me. I finish the outer coat of feathers, leaving the chest for later. I go back upstairs and make a sandwich and drink the cold, black coffee still left in the pot from this morning. I like it best that way. I'm excited about Rose coming but I'm trying to remain calm and focused on the task at hand. I'll take out a few more skinheads before she gets here; soon that house on Bingham Street will be cleaned out. I'm hoping that with the death of Bradley Wilson, they'll lose direction and scatter back to the backwoods.

I spend the rest of the day cleaning. I want the house to be immaculate for when Rose gets here. I'm going to lay low until she does, no need to take any unnecessary risks and screw the whole plan up. It's a 9 hour drive from Iowa, a straight shot to Detroit. I wish businesses were open so I could take her out on the town. It's been six long years. We've video chatted a few times, and talked on the phone a bunch, but our main method of communication has been texts and Facebook messages. I can't wait to finally meet her.

The days pass slowly until I finally receive a message from Rose saying she's leaving now. It's 8 AM, so she'll arrive by 5 PM at the latest. I wish her a safe journey and ask her if she's sure about doing this, and she assures me that her mind is made up. Okay, I say. You can have my bed, and yes, I washed the sheets. I'll take the couch. See you when you get here, I tell her. She says that she loves me and can't wait to see me, and that she'll be there soon.

I finish up the chest feathers of the golden eagle. I'm going to give it to Rose as a gift. She loves birds. I go back upstairs and listen to the *Ghost Dog* soundtrack while oiling my blades. I sit in Dad's chair and look out the window; a few Nazis coming and going, probably to the grocery store. I wonder what those pigs eat. Probably lawn fertilizer. Speaking of lawns, it's mid-May and the grass is getting long. I need gas for the mower. I'll walk to the gas station and get a can tomorrow. Saint Nick shows up at the door at 2 to deliver the daily garbage, and we chat about how the neo Nazis have amped up their efforts, harassing Muslims and vandalizing their properties. Jerry Mahone is expected to arrive in town within the next few weeks to make a speech. All the wolves will be out howling their applause. Soon there will be silence.

I get anxious around 4:30 PM. I hope Rose is safe. She's going to be exhausted when she gets here. At 5:10 a big, bulky, green Dodge Ram pulls into the driveway and out steps Rose. I'm elated. I fling the front door open and run to her, grabbing her in a big bear hug. She laughs in delight. Well hello to you too, she says with a wink. Rose! I can't believe you're really here! And you're real! Real as they come, babe, she says with a grin. We look at each other and smile widely, hold hands, and go inside the house.

We talk for hours late into the night. She drinks vodka tonics and I drink NA beer, and we laugh about all the crazy things that have happened over the last six years. We really should have done this sooner, she says, and I agree. We watch TV and make fun of it and listen to music, making dirty jokes throughout it all. We feast on Buddy's Hawaiian pizza. For the first time in years, I feel happy. I tell her that and she says she feels the same way. We stare at each other intently. She's beautiful, and I normally hate beautiful things. But not Rose. We love each other and that is beautiful. She's been the one constant in my life since Mom and Dad died.

The next day we get down to making plans for the big kill. I'm supposed to go on a date with this dickhead, Rose says, and then he's going to introduce me to Wilson. I'll be wearing a dress, so it's going to be difficult to conceal a gun, but there is another option, she says. She lifts her hand and shows me a large metal ring on her finger. She opens it to show me the empty chamber inside. It's a poison ring, she says. I have two of them, one for each hand, one for each bastard. I can take out the dickhead and Wilson while we're talking and drinking. You're brilliant, I tell her. It's so simple. It just might work. When is the date? I ask her. Tomorrow night, she says. When do you have to leave? The next day, she says, and suddenly I'm overcome by a profound sense of sadness and loss.

I tell Rose that I'm not comfortable with her going out with this guy alone, but I know that I can't come or tail them because it would arouse suspicion. Trust me, she says, I know what I'm doing. I bite my lip and don't argue. I've learned over the years that any argument with Rose is futile because she's almost always right.

It bothers me that I won't be able to see what's happening; I have to sit and wait in the house and hope for the best. I don't tell Rose any of this though. I don't want to add any more stress to her life right now. I need to have faith in her. I need to trust her, like she told me to do. We spend the rest of the evening talking about other things. I want to get her mind off it until tomorrow night. Maybe we can walk to the river tomorrow afternoon. She likes fishing, and I still have my dad's old poles in the garage. I tell her this and she becomes excited, which makes me happy and pleased.

The next morning I wake to the smell of breakfast cooking. I get off the couch and go into the kitchen where I find Rose poaching eggs. She's making Eggs Benedict. I went to the grocery store earlier, she says when I ask. I made your favorite, she says. I haven't had Eggs Benedict since Dad died. I look at her in her pretty blue eyes and say thanks. I love you, she says. I love you too, Rose, I say back. We finish breakfast and I clean the dishes. Then we get the poles from the garage and head down to the river, passing the Nazi house. Rose is wearing a baseball cap and sunglasses so no one will recognize her.

We trudge through the mud and rocks and grasses til we reach the banks. Rose says that it's a lovely river, and a dark feeling comes over me. No, not Rose. I extinguish the thought like a cigarette. We fish for a couple hours but don't catch anything. Rose enjoys nature as much as I do. It was good to get outside, she says with a smile. She's always positive, even in the midst of a global pandemic. I think she's my Muse, or my Valkyrie.

We go back to the house and watch cartoons all day until it's time for her to leave. She goes upstairs to change her clothes and comes down wearing a stunning red gown. How do I look? she asks. You're gonna give that damned Nazi a boner, I say, and she laughs. She does her hair up and puts on makeup until she's radiant. She's radiant even without makeup. When I ask her if she has a weapon, she lifts her gown to show me a stiletto strapped to her thigh. That's my girl! I say, and she flashes me a wicked grin.

Two hours later she leaves, and I'm a nervous wreck. I immediately call Alphonse and tell him the situation and he says he'll be right over. Five minutes later he pulls up in his big truck. We gotta do a stakeout, I tell him, and I give him Wilson's address. He plugs it into his GPS and we pull out of the driveway. We listen to the Wu Tang Clan on our way to Westland. We come within three block of Wilson's house and park at the curb. I have my phone in case Rose calls. I've instructed her to call me at the first sign of trouble. Twenty minutes later we see a black Mustang turn the corner followed by Rose's green Ram. This is it, I tell Alphonse. We sit and wait. The phone remains silent. We sit for 45 minutes then I get a text. It's Rose. The text reads, Mission accomplished. I tell her to meet me at my house.

Rose, Alphonse, and I go into my house and sit. She's intoxicated having committed her first murder, her first double murder. She tells us that she and the dickhead Nazi went to the liquor store to buy 40's and then to sit in the park and she was forced to listen to his Aryan bullshit. He kept telling Rose that she was his Aryan princess. He was drunk. Then they left to meet Wilson. Rose says that he was a friendly old gentleman and that she would have never suspected him of being a bigot, though he was. The three of them sat and talked for about twenty minutes, then Wilson asked Rose to make him a Manhattan.

He had a full bar in the living room where they sat. One for me too, said the dickhead. Rose poured the bourbon and sweet vermouth, adding a twist of arsenic from each of her rings. She returned with the drinks and they continued their conversation about patriotism. The dickhead gulped his down, but Wilson drank slowly in sips, occasionally setting his glass down on a doily. In ten minutes his drink was gone. The two Nazis started complaining about not feeling well, and their eyelids kept getting heavier as their pulses slowed. Rose wanted to make sure she finished the job so while they sat helpless she removed the stiletto from her thigh and slashed their throats.

Atta girl! I exclaim. She's a badass woman, boss, says Alphonse. Rose is all smiles. But she knows she can't stay in town for long. She tells me that she'll leave tomorrow morning. Alphonse and I say goodbye and he gets in his truck and vanishes into the night. Rose, I say, I have something for you. I'll be right back. I go down to the basement to retrieve the golden eagle. I hold it behind my back to surprise her and then present it to her. She gasps. It's beautiful! she says. Is this really for me? Yes, Rose, for a job well done, and because I love you and stuff, I say. Aww, you're such a sweetheart. You're my husband in hell, Rose says.

We spend the next hour listening to music and dancing crazily throughout the house. We eat junk food, play board games, watch old cartoons from our childhoods. This is bliss, I tell myself. But soon it will be gone. Our goofy little party is bittersweet; we both know she must leave in the morning. It's getting late. I put "Whistle Down the Wind" by Tom Waits on the stereo and we dance together slowly, enjoying the moment, enjoying each other. Tomorrow she'll be gone, but for this brief moment in time, we are together.

At 7 AM Rose is packing up. I help her load up her truck. Get the fuck outta here, I tell her. I plan to, you old dog, she says with a smile. Rose gets in her truck and I walk to the driver's side window and she rolls it down. Be safe, I tell her. Call or text at any time if there's any trouble. Stop worrying so much, she says. You're such a worry wart! I laugh and we kiss, then she pulls out of the driveway, drives down the street, and is gone. It feels like I've just stabbed myself with the Damascus through my own heart. She'll go back to Iowa, to the cornfields, and be with her boyfriend. They're good together, I tell myself, I don't want to muck any of that up. Her happiness is my only concern. For a moment I wish that I believed in hell because there we could be together forever, as we've promised each other. But there is no life after death. Mom and Dad are gone. I might never see Rose again.

2:35 PM. Saint Nick is at the door dancing with excitement. Did you hear the news? he asks. What news? I say. Someone killed Old Man Wilson! Poisoned him then slashed his throat! He's dead as a doornail! So what's next? I ask. The National Socialists are in disarray! Wilson was their Christ! They don't know their ass from their elbow now, if they ever did. The Movement is without its leader, and is quickly weakening! Watch it on the news! he says. I will tonight, I tell him. He hands me the junk. I go inside and throw it in the can.

I didn't think I'd get this depressed after Rose left. We'll still talk online, but having her here was magical. Her company made me feel more at peace than any of the killings I've done. Mom and Dad would have loved her too. She says she loves me and refers to me as her hell husband, but I know it's just platonic. That's okay with me; I was born to be a bachelor, but she is my best friend and a woman. She would make an excellent wife. Just not my wife. I gotta get over this before I work myself up into a funk. There's nothing to do now though thanks to Rose; the Nazis will be gone soon, and things will go back to normal, quietly racist. What's left for me to do now?

4 PM. Laying on the couch, staring at the ceiling again. I've been like this for a couple hours. I hate being human. I hate being just another upright walking cow in the herd. I thought I was doing right by my own code, but killing brought me no pleasure compared to Rose. I didn't even realize my feelings for her ran this deep. I knew that we were great friends, but being in her company, I felt something else. That prickling sensation I feel when I remember Mom and Dad. I thought I had erased them, painted over them with blood, but this whole experience has only taught me that my love for her is real but will never be realized. I should call the doctor and tell him to pump up the antidepressants. There's a pill for everything.

Maybe I could knock off a few dog walkers and fishermen, like in the old days. But I fear that it will just feel empty and hollow. I always said I'd rather be feared than loved, but I don't feel that way anymore. I just want Rose. I want us to eat junk food together and watch old cartoons. I want us to run through fields wearing armor and do battle with imaginary monsters. I want us to be together. Not sexually, but something more than friendship. Something bordering on romantic. I don't know if people have those kinds of relationships. I think my fantasy is antiquated. I'm an old-fashioned fool. But that's what Rose loves about me. It's all so confusing.

They're talking about the Wilson murder on the news and the immediate effect it's had on the National Socialist Movement. Sounds like they're floundering now that their voice is gone. He was an evil bastard but he was a brilliant evil bastard. Not too many Nazis like him left in America. Rose did a flawless job. She even used a fake name and identity so they'll never find her. She's safe. I'll wait for her to contact me to let me know she's okay. I don't want to be overbearing. She's probably a bundle of emotions right now. I hope she doesn't regret doing what she did. She saved this whole community, myself included.

At 10 I get a message from Rose. She's safe at home. She says how great it was to finally meet me and that she loves me even more now. She says I changed her. How? I ask. Killing those two bastards was such a thrill that I want more of it, she says. Plenty of dumb cows in Iowa, she says, probably even more than in Michigan. They're all simple minded ignorant redneck racist farmer peasants, she says. You've inspired me to start knocking them off, she says. Rose, I say, it's not a good idea. It's extremely risky and I was lucky not to get caught. Please don't do this. Too late, she says. I shot a man two hours ago and left him in the cornfields. No one will find him in there. The Cornfield Killer! You gave me the idea! I stare at the screen and shake my head. I didn't mean for this to happen.

Rose, I say, you changed me too. I don't want to kill anymore. I love you. I just want us to be together. We are together, she says, like Bonnie and Clyde, she says. I don't want it to be this way, Rose. I want to retire and be with you. Please don't take this path and make the same mistake I did. Nah, she says, you got me hooked. I'm going to pick them off from my front porch and put em in the corn. It's perfect, she says. You're going to be my mentor, she says. Rose, I don't want to be anyone's mentor, especially yours. You're not a killer. Don't go through with this, I say. Babe, she says, I love you but I'm gonna do what I'm gonna do. Don't try to change me, please, she says. I should have known something like this would happen. It was bound to end in disaster.

I stay up late thinking about the current state of affairs. Global pandemic, holy wars, serial killers on the loose. I wasn't expecting copycats, certainly not sweet Rose. She's always had it in her though, I suppose, the disgust and contempt that I once ate and drank like steak and NA beer. I know there's no use trying to change her mind, so I'll just be there for her and hopefully my love will show her the road back to sanity. She's like a teenaged boy who's just had his first orgasm; she got a taste and now she wants to eat the whole pie. I can't stop her. I'm not going to the police; that's out of the question for a variety of reasons, the most important being that I love her.

7 AM the next morning. Just going through the motions. I don't what to say to Rose anymore. She's a different person, infected by the same insanity that I was for so long. I don't know when or if she'll snap out of it. They'll never find the bodies in those cornfields, and she has a truck so she's mobile. Lack of transportation was my biggest weakness, until I found Alphonse. And even then I had to pay him off every time to stay quiet. Now he's in on it too so I don't know what's going to happen with that. I like to think that I can trust him but I might have to take him out if worse comes to worst.

1:24 PM. Saint Nick at the door. He tells me that the neo Nazis are moving out of the house down the street. They're all packing up. The virus is still rampant and people aren't leaving their houses, he says. No Rouge River Killer news, he says. Seems like the murders have dried up, thankfully, he says. I thank him for the update and the catalogues and close the door.

Looks like I'm retired. Now my job is to stop Rose. All I have at my disposal are words, but words are powerful. I don't want to lecture her though. That would be completely hypocritical since I'm still disgusted by the fat cows myself. Maybe if I can convince her to target a disposable group, instead of randomly killing, that will set her on the right track. She's a beautiful woman, so I'm sure she gets a lot of unwanted attention from guys. Maybe she could kill rapists or pedophiles. Sexual predators. I'll run the idea by her when she texts me.

I'm eating a sandwich and online window shopping when I get a message from Rose. It's 3 PM and she's already killed five people. Shot them in the head, good and dead! she says. I don't scold her. I suggest that she be more selective in her targets. Not a bad idea, she says, but I still love popping these dumb hicks and putting them in the corn. Just think about it, I say, you'd be doing some good while getting relief from the urges. Yeah, that's true, she says. You're probably right, I should go after the bad guys. I know plenty of women, myself included, who have been victimized by men, starting at an early age. I'll lure them in close then cut their throats with my stiletto. That's good, Rose, I say. Have your vengeance. You'll be famous. Can't wait! she says.

Maybe I'll go back to my writing, I always enjoyed that. It would be amusing to me if I were to put this all down on paper one day. *Memoirs of the Rouge River Killer*, I like the sound of that. I would have to fictionalize it though, otherwise it'd be a confession and I won't be spending any time in prison if I can help it. What to do about Rose is the question. Maybe over time I can wean her off the murder intoxication. Right now she's green and excited. Hopefully the jadedness will sink in as it did with me. I'll continue to guide her for now, and slowly my words will sink in. Maybe then we can be together.

I get a text from Rose. She says she had planned to go to some hick bar to lure in prey but forgot that everything is still closed. It's going to be hard tracking down the creeps, she says, if there are no public places open. You'll figure it out, I tell her. There's no sense in senseless violence; it's like shooting a gun, I tell her. You have to be precise and aim for the target. This makes sense to her and she agrees. I'm glad I'm getting through to her. This is a dangerous game.

I start writing, beginning with the first outbreak of the virus. I set the story in another city in another state, and change all the names. I'm writing about my parents. I write two pages about them then lay on the couch. Mom's hugs, Dad's laugh. I feel like I'm about to have a breakdown. The memories are too painful, and I can't properly focus because of my concern for Rose. I need a distraction. I find *The Dark Crystal* on Netflix and pay close attention to the puppetry and backgrounds. If I'm visually stimulated, I have an easier time focusing and maintaining concentration. I like the Mystics best. I wish I had three arms. I could eat a sandwich with two hands and scratch my sack with the third.

At 6 PM I write a few paragraphs about the neighborhood and the herd of cattle. Then I turn on the public radio station and listen to classical music. I wish I could read; I was once a voracious reader but the illness ruined all that. The doctor says that part of the illness is cognitive decline, which is why I can't read and why my memory is so bad. I don't even remember the people I killed. Everything before Rose's arrival is hazy in my mind. I mostly remember quiet evenings with Mom and Dad. Playing games, watching TV, being a family.

A news report comes on over the radio and the reporter says that plans to build a new mosque in town are in the works, that the cathedral is undergoing restoration. The community is rebuilding itself, I think, that's good. Still not a fan of any religion but at least they're not shooting each other anymore. Positive steps are being taken to restore what was lost. Maybe I'll go for a walk this evening. I'll only carry my pocket knife.

At 8 PM I head out into the neighborhood. It's late May, the trees are in full leaf. Gotta cut the grass, I remind myself. Gotta clean up the window boxes too, for Mom. I walk the sidewalks in darkness, glimpses of the past resurfacing in my worn out memory. I buried a body in those bushes, I think. There was an old man smoking a pipe. He's gone now.

I head down to the river, where I fished with Rose. I sit on a rock on the banks and watch the moving black water, wondering how many bodies are sitting at the river bottom, or have floated downriver and out to the lake. I put those bodies there. I was a murderer, but that's all over now. Now I have to reform Rose before she gets caught. It's going to be difficult to do from a distance. I wish we had mutual friends that I could call upon for help. But she and I only have each other.

I walk back home through the night, the streetlights casting long shadows behind my figure and the trees. No one is out on the streets but me. The cows are safe in their homes, doing their cow activities. Happy little consumers. My contempt has turned to irritated tolerance, and I've been feeling less alien in the neighborhood, though I still can't relate to anyone here except for Saint Nick and Alphonse. I think Alphonse lives downtown. I'll have to call him and make sure everything's good between us. He strikes me as a man of his word, and he hates the Nazis, so I think he was happy to help. Still, I don't entirely know if I can trust him to keep his mouth shut, especially if he's questioned. I'll talk with him again soon.

I reach my house at a little after 9 PM. I wonder if Rose has texted me. I go inside to the dark living room and sit on the couch, checking my phone. No new messages. I go online to see if she's active but she's not. I send her a text to ask how she's doing and a few minutes later she responds. Doing the devil's work, she says happily. Today I paid a visit to my old co-worker and her abusive boyfriend. She would always come into the diner with bruises and almost got fired for it. She and I chatted while he got drunk and watched football, then I introduced him to my stiletto, she tells me. I stabbed that fucker in the throat, she says, and we bagged up the body and dumped it in the dumpster. Chelsea feels safer now, and there won't be any more bruises, she says. I tell her good work, stay focused on the bad guys. You got it, boss! I love ya, beeboo! she says. I love you too, Rose, I tell her.

I watch old cartoons for the rest of the night. I can't stop thinking about Rose, and how she's changed, and if my feelings for her now are the same as they once were. As far as I know she still has a boyfriend, though I don't know how long that will last now that she's killing people. Not that it matters. It's probably best that I don't see her in person again; she would eventually leave, and I would be overcome with melancholy again. Still, I long for those few brief nights we were together. It made me feel human when the hatred left my heart. I only want the same for her.

My beard's getting long again but I like the look. Rose does too, she's told me. I think I'll cut the lawn today. I need gas for the mower. I walk to the gas station at the end of the street and buy a can, fill it, and walk back home. The sun is shining and everything is green. I walk up the driveway to the garage and gas up the mower. Then I get to work. I hate mowing the lawn because it make me feel exposed and vulnerable, but my mind is on Rose. The noise of the mower and the smell of the cut grass offends my ears and nostrils, but I manage to get the front and back done in about a half hour. I put the mower back in the garage. Summer will be here soon. The heat, the sweat, the bloated cows in tank tops in the streets. But I don't feel the itch anymore. I just want to be left alone to work on my woodcarving projects and hopefully guide Rose out of the darkness.

I go back inside the house and write for a few hours. Mostly about Rose and our friendship. Six years is a long time, and it feels like I've known her my whole life. I take a break and send her a text. Two more hits, she says. Both domestic violence cases. It's a small town so word of that shit spreads fast, she says. I poisoned their beers. I'm making house calls now; a girlfriend will call me and I'll stop by for a visit and take out her piece of shit boyfriend. It's all I can do, she says. With everything closed I can't pick guys up at the bars and lure them back to the house, so I have to go to them. I'm only targeting bad guys now, like you told me to, she says. I don't feel so bad hearing this. Guys who beat their women are the lowest of the low. They deserve Rose's vengeance.

When I tell Rose that I've retired, she's disappointed. It's your fault, I tell her laughing. You restored my faith in humanity haha, I say. Who me? she says innocently. Yes, woman, you, I say. I had such a great time with you that it made me rethink things. I haven't had fun like that in years. You gave me hope that I'll feel happy again, I tell her. You're my hell husband, she says, I love you. That's when she tells me that she and Tom broke up. He couldn't handle what I was doing. He was always a pussy boy, she says. You're my demon lord, she says. You inspired me to clean up this cesspool. You're my mentor. I love you beeboo, she says. I love you too, I say. Just get it out of your system and maybe one day things will change for you too. I'll be here waiting, if you decide to come back. I will, she says.

I call Alphonse. I want all my bases covered. I dial him up and he answers. Are we good? I say. Yeah, we're good boss. Don't worry about a thing. We did a good thing the other night, the three of us. The city's going back to normal. No more violence, he says. Yes, I say, no more violence. Thank you, Alphonse, I say. No problem, boss, he says. Anytime you need a ride, you call me, and I won't charge you extra. I want to help you clean up this city, he says. Will do, I say, thanks again. I'll be in touch.

Saint Nick shows up at 2 with the usual junk. He tells me that things have settled down since the Wilson slaying, that soon things will be back to normal in Viral World. I ask him about his family and he says they're all healthy, staying indoors and keeping safe from the virus. I tell him to be safe himself, take whatever precautions he can. He says he is; he's learning to practice social distancing and is washing his hands now constantly. That's good, I say. Same time tomorrow? Nick says. I'll be here, I say.

I draw a hot bath, sit in the tub, and think my thoughts. I wonder what Nick would think of me if he knew that I was the one behind all the killings. I felt bad for scaring him, but I never would have harmed him. I wonder what Rose is doing. Probably solving another domestic violence dispute. She can't go on killing her friends' abusive boyfriends; she's going to get caught. She lives in a small town where everyone talks to everyone and knows everything about everybody else. She's told me she's never had a problem with the police in the past; she had family on the local force for years, and she's already well-known in town as the local eccentric. I don't think anyone would suspect her to be a serial killer. She could fool any man with her charm.

Who am I now that I'm no longer a killer? This question has been bothering me for days. Ever since Rose left I've been reexamining myself and my beliefs. I still don't believe in good and evil; that's an oversimplification. For a long time I believed that the more accurate dichotomy was order and chaos, that I was an agent of chaos as the Rouge River Killer, that I restored order through Rose, but now she's killing people too. She's killing bad people, that's good, but I really want to put some distance between myself and killing. Maybe the true dichotomy is well-being and harm. I'll have to think on it more later.

I dry myself off and drain the bathwater, go in the kitchen, and cook two sausages with peppers and onions. I sit and eat at the table, doodling on the junk mail. I call this abstract piece, "Ballpoint Pen Nightmare." I crumple it up and throw it In the trash, along with the rest of the junk. I have hours to kill before bedtime, and I've got to get out of my head for a while, so I hook up the old Super Nintendo and play *Earthbound*. It's my favorite game, along with *Street Fighter 2*. I used to be able to beat Bison with Ryu using only the hard kick. That was years ago, when things were simpler.

Rose texts me at 8 PM. Two more dead, drunken, abusive slobs. One of them gave her friend a black eye and a broken arm. He now has a gaping hole in his throat, Rose tells me. I try to act encouraging.

I go to bed at midnight. At 3 AM I'm woken by the sound of my phone ringing. It's Rose. I gotta get outta Dodge, and fast, she says. A hit went wrong. I'll explain when I get there. You're coming here now? I ask. Yes, if that's okay. I gotta get outta Iowa now and I have nowhere else to go, she says. Ok, Ok, I say, I'll be waiting for you.

I get out of bed and immediately go to work cleaning the house. I dust, mop, scrub. I wash and dry my sheets so she'll have a clean bed to sleep in. I don't know how long she'll be here but she'll be here by noon. I eat a quick breakfast and get back to cleaning the bathroom. Scrubbing the bathroom floor is no different than cleaning the basement floor after dismembering a body, not as messy but it's still work. I finish everything by 7 AM, lay down on the couch, and pass out for a few hours.

I wake at 11 AM. Rose will be here in an hour. I'm excited to see her. I'm curious what happened. Rose never makes mistakes, so the foul up couldn't have been her doing. I pace the wooden floor for an hour sucking on lozenges. At 12:35 the Ram pulls into the driveway and Rose steps out. She looks exhausted and frantic at the same time. I open the front door to greet her and she gives me a huge hug. She starts to cry. Beeboo, I fucked up, she says. Don't worry, tell me inside, I say, and I lead her through the doorway, holding her hand.

I sit her down on the couch and tell her to tell me everything. I got a call from a friend, she says, her boyfriend knocked her around the night before and she wanted him out of the picture. When I got to the apartment it was just the two of them and a case of beer. I put poison in the boyfriend's can but he set it down on the table and my friend accidentally picked it up and drank it. She's dead! I killed my friend! Rose says. I try to calm her down. It wasn't your fault, Rose, I tell her, it was an accident. What happened next? I ask. Nothing! Rose says. I got the hell out of there and called you! I can't go back. I don't know what I'm going to do, she says. We'll figure it out, I say. You can stay here as long as you need to. Thank you, beeboo, I don't know what I'd do without you.

We're going to have fun together, I tell her. She weakly smiles. I can tell she's still upset about the death of her friend.

When the mail comes at 2 PM I introduce Rose to Saint Nick. They like each other immediately. They're both likable people. The three of us chat for a while, about the virus, the holy war, the killings. We try to keep our spirits up by joking about all of it. It's the Crapocalypse! Nick says. Rose and I laugh. Nick hands me the mail and we say our goodbyes and I close the front door. Rose goes to the kitchen to make lunch. I sit on the couch and think my thoughts.

It's like we're a couple now, only we aren't. We both love each other like mad, but we're not together. We live together now, but we sleep apart. I'm afraid to ask Rose to clarify the situation. I want to know how she feels about us, about me. I should just content myself being friends. I'm lucky just to know her. Still, a part of me wishes for something more.

Rose walks into the living room with sandwiches and we sit on the couch and watch *The Last Unicorn*. We both joke about the corny soundtrack, but we love the movie. Rose says she's feeling a little better now that she knows that it was an accident and could have happened to anyone. I put my arm around her and she doesn't mind. She snuggles close. I hold her for a few minutes and then we go back to watching the movie. I don't know if she wants me to make a move, and I'm not willing to risk offending her. So we sit and watch, holding hands. It's a strange moment for me, and probably for her too.

After the movie ends we continue to sit and she strikes up a conversation about favorite things from our childhoods. She says that she was obsessed with Brian Jacques' *Redwall* series, and I tell her that I used to read those books too. Yes! she says, and we high five. I tell her how I used to love reading *Ranger Rick* magazine when I was a boy, and she says she loved that magazine. Two for two, I say, and she smiles a big smile. She asks me if I would hold her again and I do, feeling her warmth against my own. I kiss her on the neck and she turns her head to kiss me on the mouth. She pulls a blanket over us and we cuddle on the couch. I am happy.

We eat a quick dinner then go for an evening walk. The sun is setting as we walk. Everything is green. We hold hands and make our way down the street. Who would guess all the blood we've spilled between us. We crack a few jokes as we walk, but we mostly remain silent, holding hands. It's beautiful here, Rose says. You make it beautiful, I tell her. She blushes and smiles. I kiss her on the forehead and she hugs me. I love you, she says. I love you too, Rose.

Later that night Rose is kicking my ass at *Street Fighter 2*. On the stereo the *Braveheart* soundtrack blares. It's one of Rose's favorites. She's a warrior and loves battle music. We should have been born in The Dark Ages, though the current Age is pretty dark. She tells me about all the sick people in Iowa and how she felt surrounded by death there. I ask her if she feels better here and she says yes. I tell her she's my jungle queen and she says I'm her demon lord and we both laugh. At 1 AM she goes upstairs to my room. I go to sleep on the couch.

In the morning we're both up eating breakfast. I cooked Dad's potatoes and onions for Rose and she loves it. Would you like to learn how to carve wood today, babe? I ask her. Sure! she says. After breakfast, I say. Once we're finished cleaning up, we go downstairs to the basement. I show her the carving station. She looks around, admiring all the wood spirits and gnomes on Dad's work desk and everywhere else. I sit her down with me at the station and show her the knives and chisels. I show her the blocks of bass wood. Then I start chipping away at a block, talking to her while I'm carving, until I've roughed out the form of a small bird. Let me try! she says, and I hand her a block of wood and the carving knife. She whittles away with enthusiasm until there's a face staring out from the block. You're a natural born carver, I say. I had a good teacher, she replies with a wink.

We go back upstairs and take our pills and drink coffee. She's wearing my clothes. I hope you don't mind, Rose says, I didn't have time to pack. I don't mind, I say. We'll order you some nice clothes. We can pick them out together. We go online and look at Etsy and other vintage clothing retailers. Rose likes the retro look. Her fashion sense could be described as post-apocalyptic military grunge chic, which is similar to my own when I'm not wearing my normie costume. I could use some new clothes too since I've lost weight, so we look at men's clothing too. We each order a few outfits. She thanks me for everything I've done for her. You're my best friend, I say, hoping to get a reaction. You're my hell husband, she replies with a smile.

We watch a Pixar movie that night. Rose loves 3D animation, but I prefer the traditional stuff. We sit on the couch and cuddle up close, and I start to feel the feelings again. I'm wondering if she's feeling them too. I give her a smooch on the cheek and she grins. I'm watching the movie! she says. You know you like it, I say, and give her a tickle. She laughs until we're wrestling on the floor and I'm on top of her. Then we realize what we're doing and look at each other and laugh. We get up and finish the movie, then chat about everything and nothing for a few hours. I ask Rose what her favorite color is. Depends on the context, she says. Red for clothes, black for electronics, electric blue for cars and trucks. Who's your celebrity crush, I ask her. Danny DeVito, she says with a grin.

A few days later our clothes arrive. Rose and I have a fashion show and model our new outfits for each other. You look hawt, beeboo, she tells me. Girl, you're so fine you're on my mind all of the time, I say back. We laugh. Rose tells me that she wants to tell me something. The last week with you has been magical, she says, and I'm feeling happy for the first time in a long time. I don't have the itch anymore, she says. That's great news, I tell her. I've been waiting for this day.

I think we should retire, I say, later that night. We can do arts and crafts, and watch TV, eat junk food, and go on adventures together. That'd be way more fun, I tell her. I think we're in agreement, Rose says. I'm tired of all the bloodshed, and I have nowhere to go, no home to return to. I like staying here with you. I like your house and yard. I like being with you. You're my best friend, my hell husband, my demon lord, she says.

Wanna get married in Hell still? I ask Rose. Of course! Why do you ask? There's a town here in Michigan called Hell. We could get hitched there, if you wanted. Rose looks at me and smiles. Beeboo, are you proposing? Are ya gonna make me take a knee? I ask. She turns around on the couch and grabs me. We kiss long and hard on the mouth. I always wanted it to be this way, she says. Six long years; I knew it was going to be you all along. So that's a yes? I ask. Yes! You dumbass! Of course! We hold each other for a few long minutes, feeling each other breathe. Just being. In the same space, in the same time, two grains of stardust reunited in the vast emptiness.

www.ingramcontent.com/pod-product-compliance
Lightning Source LLC
Chambersburg PA
CBHW050845180626
46814CB00007B/2625